I0695014

JENNY POWELL

Take the Sea

Jenny Powell

ISBN-13: 978-1-965352-95-3

Take The Sea will utterly delight lovers of church history. Through a seamless dual-timeline tale, Jenny Powell weaves together the storylines of John Wesley and Hope, a modern-day woman dealing with past trauma. Powell approaches the results of tragedy with sensitivity and grace. This well-researched story will both inform and inspire readers to look to Jesus as their anchor in the storm.

~Sarah Hanks, award-winning author of the Mercy series and Sister in Arms collection

Jenny Powell's novel *Take The Sea* is an inspirational story of overcoming traumatic experiences of fear by Divine grace, professional counseling, and unexpected sources of encouragement. The story focuses on Hope, a wife and mother of two children and who nearly drowned at age 13, and interweaves her journey of recovery with John Wesley, an icon of religious faith in Christian history, who faced his own fears of the sea during his trip to America in the 1700s. For those interested in John Wesley and his journey of faith, Powell brings to life with creative retellings of several events in his life. I highly recommend this novel to anyone seeking healing and hope in their lives, who want to experience God's restoring presence in their hearts.

~Dr. Mark K. Olson, editor, Wesley Scholar Website (www.wesleyscholar.com)

What a fun book to read! Entertaining, enlightening, and empowering all at the same time. It starts strong and only gets better. Dr. Jenny Powell uses her gifts as a believer, doctor, writer, and researcher to pull off wonderful work. Great job. My recommendation: take the time to *Take The Sea*!

~Chris Schneider VP at LakeTV and author of *Angel Dreams & Starting Your Career in Broadcasting*

With its seamless blend of historical insight and heartfelt storytelling, *Take the Sea* is a deeply moving reminder that fear doesn't have the final word—faith does. Through parallel journeys of John Wesley and a modern-day woman named Hope, the story gently leads readers to see how trusting God in the face of fear brings lasting freedom.

~Ruth Schmeckpeper, author and Semi-finalist ACFW Genesis contest

I have been a licensed psychologist in the State of Missouri since 1989. I practice CBT and have treated patients with PTSD, anxiety disorders, and various phobias. I completely read Take the Sea and enjoyed every minute of it. Dr. Powell did a fantastic job with the psychological content. The therapy sessions were very realistic. Her descriptions of Hope's thoughts and feelings were quite appropriate. I am a Christian with a background similar to the characters in Take the Sea. Their story was so familiar and accurate that by the end, they had become friends that I did not want to leave.

~Mary K Richardson, Ph.D.

Dedication

This book is dedicated to everyone who has ever needed to hear or read the following words from the mouth of God: FEAR NOT.

To my granddaughters: Cady, M.Vera, Bea, Virginia, and Charlotte. #beinggrandmaisthebest

And to Loretta Matthews. Thanks for making one of the most difficult decisions a mother ever has to make. I love you.

Chapter One

A dream is a fragment of life, broken off at both ends.
John Wesley, Sermon 121

Hope Gerard
Wyckles, Missouri
Mid-April

One moment, Hope is in the boat. The next, she is immersed, the lake engulfing her.

The sounds of the depths roar in her ears. Her arms frantically push against the swirling darkness, and the sudden cold of the water presses against her. She sinks. *Which way is up?*

Hope kicks her aching legs slowly. Needing air, she fights the urge to gulp the cold water, to extinguish the burning in her chest.

Her heartbeat slows. *Think.* Bubbles. Bubbles rise. The urge to breathe is too strong, and panic rises once again. Her nostrils are full of water.

Look up.

Where is up? She sweeps her head from side to side.

Look up.

She tilts her head backward. Through the darkness, shimmering above, a beam of light diffuses through the water. Hope kicks, reaching towards it.

Warm, strong hands encompass her body, forcing her toward the surface, accelerating her ascent against the pressure. The light radiates above her. She is almost there.

The hands leave her as she breaks the surface of the water. Gasping for air, her wet hair is pasted to her face.

"Nana!" Hope cries out, bolting upright in her bed.

Her ice-cold body shakes. Her teeth chatter and she longs for warmth. Blurry red digits glow from their bedroom clock. She blinks, clearing her vision. Four forty-four. She slows her panting and wraps her arms around herself.

Soft paws pad their way into her bedroom. Shadow lays his dark head on the edge of the bed. When he whines, Hope pats the bed next to her. He climbs, one cautious inch at a time, and lays a big paw on her lap. She hugs him to her chest.

Hope can make out the outline of her husband's body under the covers, his back to her. There was a time when Matthew sat up next to her, holding her, brushing her hair away from her face, murmuring soft, calming words. His slow, steady exhalations assure her he is deep in sleep, that he slept soundly through her wild awakening, her gasps, her cry in the night. She knows she ought not to blame him, that every year, as the anniversary creeps closer, it is always the same. Same dream, same fear, same cry. She ought not to blame him for his desensitization to her terror.

But she does. She resents his ability to sleep through her yearly crisis, no matter how many years it has been.

Hope hugs her black lab tighter and sobs into his warm fur.

Hope had given up on any more rest, terrified of falling back asleep and returning to the dream, so she had waited with swollen eyelids until the sun crept over the horizon.

Matthew's form is still, and his breathing steady. Hope eases out of bed, and Shadow lifts his dark head as she tiptoes across the carpet to their master bath. She gently latches the door behind her, then leans wearily on the cool marble countertop. Puffy, red-rimmed eyes peer back at her in the mirror. That's what a night full of crying does.

She tests the temperature of the stream from the shower head. Maybe its steamy heat will chase away the cold fear that has failed to leave her. She steps gingerly into the shower, her back to the water, and takes in deep breaths as the droplets sting the skin between her shoulder blades. As she washes, she is careful to avoid water on her head or face. No time to wash and dry her hair on a Sunday morning. Plus, there's the creepy goosebumps she gets when water runs down her face.

Thoughts of Nana flood her, the only mother figure she has ever known. Her only memories of her real mother are mere shadows. Hope was very young when her mother died in a car accident, and only glimpses of the woman remained. She often questions if her memories are genuine, or if her young mind had formed them around the pictures Nana shared as Hope sat on Nana's lap, the heavy photo album perched on her knees.

There were no pictures of Hope's unknown father, and Nana never spoke of him. Whenever Hope would ask about him, the most Nana would comment on was how he must have given Hope her stunning skin tone. Papa would only grunt and change the subject.

As Hope dries off, the steam covering the mirror also settles on her prickly skin. She slips on her robe and eases open the door, the cooler air hitting her like a wall.

Matthew is propped up in bed, his reading glasses perched on his nose, his worn Bible open and resting on his trunk. His dark hair is tousled, some gray sprinkled about his temples.

He lifts his head from his reading. "Hey, hon." He frowns. "You look like you've been up all night. Are you alright?"

Hope fights the desire to fall onto the bed next to him, her lids heavy. But she would rather not admit her fatigue and pretend that all is well. The last few years, Matthew has been increasingly irritated by her dreams, as if she had any control over them. She nears her husband and perches on the edge of the bed as he closes his Bible and gives her his attention. She indicates the Bible with a hand. "Are you reading the scripture in worship this morning?"

"Nah." He removes his glasses. "Going over the

scripture for my class this morning." Matthew teaches the high school Sunday School at their church, leading a dozen kids into a deeper understanding of God's word every week.

She takes a deep breath. *Maybe I should gently remind him. Perhaps he will understand without me having to say much.* "I didn't sleep well. This time of year, you know."

Hope flinches as his thick brows draw down, and under his moustache, his lips press together

"You had the dream again." He isn't asking a question.

Hope nods. She holds in threatening tears. She doesn't want to break down in front of him. Sometimes, she questions if her tears aren't what has widened the gap that has gradually spanned between them. If she could manage a brave face for him, maybe he would return to the playful young man he was when they first married. He'd become so serious the last few years.

Matthew sighs and rubs his eyes with the heels of his hands. "Did you leave me enough hot water?"

Her chin drops, and any warmth left from her shower drains away. "Seriously, Matthew?"

She stands, her hands shaking. Hope clasps them to stifle the tremor.

"What? Am I supposed to be surprised?" Matthew throws back the covers. "Instead of getting better every year, it's getting worse." He shakes his head. "I don't think that's normal."

She tears her gaze from her husband, afraid to speak for fear of a trembling voice. Matthew swings his legs over the bed and plants his feet on the floor.

"You'd best get dressed and wake the kids while I

get ready." He shuffles past her toward the bathroom as she studies his receding back.

With her eight-year-old daughter anchored between her knees, Hope drags a hairbrush that may as well be made of lead through the tangled mess of blond hair.

"Ow!"

Her daughter pulls her head away.

"Samantha, you've got to hold still. You can't go to church as if you recently hopped out of bed." Hope forcefully repositions her daughter's crown.

"Oh, Mom, you know nobody's gonna be there this morning. Easter was last week!"

She separates her daughter's brushed hair into three parts. "Now, you don't know that." Hope tilts her head in wonder that her youngest is so observant of the habits of their small-town church. "It only seems that way when the out-of-town family members attend on Easter morning. Makes the following Sunday appear empty in comparison."

"I hope Frankie will be there today." Her daughter drops her head toward her lap.

"Head up, Samantha. Isn't she Joey's sister?" Hope grabs a hair tie from the counter and wraps it around the end of the braid.

"Yeah, their mom sometimes has to work on Sunday mornings. Are you done?"

Hope drops her heavy arms on her legs, regretting her forcefulness. She knows she shouldn't take out her fatigue and angst on her children. She leans over and kisses the top of her daughter's head, inhaling the scent of freshly shampooed hair. "Yes, let me see you."

Samantha slides from the stool, her shining blue eyes framed with light eyelashes, presenting a coy smile. For a moment, Hope warms, chasing the cold weariness to hover in the corner. She is blessed to have both her girl and Samantha's older brother. Hope grips her daughter's arms. "Pretty as a peach. Grab your shoes and let's go. I'm sure Dad and Eric are waiting."

Matthew chats during the short car ride to the church as if nothing had transpired earlier that morning. Dark-haired eleven-year-old Eric, Matthew's mini-me, grabs his sister's braid, gleeful when she cries out. Hope stares out the window, wordless, glad that they don't live far from the church. She is eager to see her best friend, who always makes her feel better. Little time passes before the Gerard family eases into the church parking lot.

The moment the four of them enter the back door of the church, Eric, ever the competitive athlete, darts for the stairs, taking them two at a time. Samantha scurries behind him. "Wait for me!"

Matthew shouts after them. "Kids, don't run!"

The glorious aroma of brewing coffee drifts about Hope as they near the kitchen, and she inhales deeply. Coffee will help her heavy heart.

Her husband holds his Bible in his armpit and sweeps the altar flowers awaiting him on the serving counter in his arms. Then he leans down and swipes a short kiss on her cheek. "Meet you in the sanctuary after Sunday School."

He is already on the stairs as she responds. "Yeah,

see you after."

Hope follows her nose and enters the kitchen. Her heart lifts at the sight of her best friend's straight back and tightly curled black hair as she measures coffee into the percolator. Debbie didn't have to do or say anything; solely being in her presence always made Hope feel better.

"You're supposed to wait for me." Hope drapes her arm around Debbie's shoulder. "Or did you forget?"

Debbie throws her head back, laughing. "Oh, Hope, you'll be late for your own funeral. This is the second batch already. Here." Debbie hands her a filled decanter and a stack of Styrofoam cups. "This is the decaf. Take these to our Sunday School room. I'll be right behind you with the fully leaded."

With her arms full, Hope enters the classroom. Debbie's husband, Jesse, attends a different class, one designed more for their age group. But she and Debbie have long opted to attend the class full of grandmothers and grandfathers. Hope finds that she learns more from them, and the older members seem to enjoy having Hope and Debbie with them.

Mr. Hamilton is already handing out books, and the round table is surrounded by their small group, whose aged eyes light up at the sight of the coffee. Hope unburdens her arms of their contents next to the coffee condiments. She sweeps a hand dramatically. "The decaf is served. Mr. Hamilton, Debbie will be right in."

"Bob," he says, nodding his grayed head.

Hope dips her chin. She could never bring herself to call him Bob, like practically everyone else. Mr. Hamilton was the principal when she was in high school. She takes her seat next to where Debbie's purse sits on an otherwise unoccupied chair, aching for a cup of the caffeinated coffee.

"Oh, Hope," Mr. Hamilton says, "you remember you will be leading the next six-week study, correct?"

"Yes, sir. I still need to order the materials."

"I was hoping you would put something together yourself. You did such a great job last time."

Hope wets her dry lips at the memory of the amount of time and effort she had poured into that study on Simon Peter. She had used the author's text as a base but stretched a six-week study into twelve. Research had always been one of her passions, and it made good use of her college degree. But she's hoping for something a little less time-consuming this go-around. And she is so tired. "That was a lot of work," Hope manages weakly.

"Oh, yes, Hope, please." Debbie is at her side, the second decanter in her hand. "You brought the material to life."

The others at the table all give similar encouragement. Hope sighs and drops her eyes to the table. She wants to take it easy this time and opens her mouth to tell them so. But when she lifts her head, she locks eyes with Evelyn. Eighty-five-year-old Evelyn was always so appreciative. Next to her sits the recently widowed Martha, whose face held hopeful expectation. Hope sighs. "You know I can't refuse you guys," Hope mutters. "For you, I suppose I'll tackle the most reverent John Wesley." She addresses Mr. Hamilton. "That's correct, isn't it?"

Months earlier, she, Debbie, and Mr. Hamilton set the curriculum for the year.

"John Wesley." Mr. Hamilton's ancient head bobs. "We wanted to start the study by Aldersgate Sunday in late May. Pastor Robert will be announcing that we are doing a study on him."

Blaming the fatigue and her current state of mind, Hope assures him she can manage six weeks of study material on the founder of Methodism. She prays she can make the content interesting. "At least it won't be another twelve-weeker."

Debbie pipes up. "What theme from his life is she supposed to focus on, Bob?"

Hope jerks her head toward her friend, whose bright amber eyes appear enlarged through her tortoise-shell glasses. Finding an inspiring and timely aspect of an otherwise dry topic will be tough enough.

"Oh, good question, Debbie."

As a lifelong Methodist, Bob Hamilton knows all about the founder of Methodism, and the class considers him an expert on the Wesleys. Hope was raised Lutheran, and she knows only what they discuss in this Sunday School class of her husband's hometown church. When they had developed the rotation, she had argued that Mr. Hamilton should be the one to lead any discussion on John Wesley. However, he had insisted that they stay on the previously agreed-upon schedule.

"I suggest we focus on his fear of death, especially since that was such a dramatic turning point for John Wesley. It would make a wonderful segue between our Lenten and Resurrection studies, and Aldersgate Sunday when Wesley had what he referred to as his conversion."

Hope has to admit, that makes sense. She closes her eyes and stretches her chin to the ceiling.

"You know," Mr. Hamilton proceeds, "when he and his brother Charles were on the ship heading to America, there was a storm at sea..."

His words fade as a roar fills Hope's ears, and her stomach churns. *A storm at sea.* The room sways back and forth. A cold sweat forms on her forehead, and she closes her eyes against nausea. She places her hands on the table and rises, as if in a dream.

"Hope?" Debbie's voice sounds far away.

"I think I'm going to be sick," she whispers.

"Let's go." Debbie steers her away from the table. They make their way toward the door, and Hope's eyes focus on a print hanging on the wall. An open hand thrusts through the water's surface, as if the artist had gazed upward toward the light breaking through the depths.

Passing into the hallway, Hope leans weakly on her friend, lunging for the women's restroom.

What have I gotten myself into?

Chapter Two

*If you are now unhappy, it is because you are in
an unnatural state.*
John Wesley, Sermon 77

Hope
Later that same morning

As Matthew backs the car out of their parking spot in the church lot, Hope wants to drop to the floor of the car. Instead, she clips her seatbelt and pretends not to see any of their church family flowing out of the building. She had spent all of Sunday School and the majority of worship time in the ladies' restroom. Halfway through the sermon, Debbie, who stayed with her the entire time, finally convinced her to slink into a pew near the back. Their movement had caused several heads to turn, including Matthew's. His look of confusion made her feel six inches tall.

The midday sun pours into their car, but can't quite warm her enough to soothe the cold that fills her. Matthew reaches for his sunglasses, and the scent of his cologne wafts toward her. The combination of sweet and musky has always been one of her favorites, but she inches away from him. Will she be able to explain her reaction in Sunday School to him?

Not a block from the church, Eric and Samantha start in at each other in the back seat.

"Stop making that noise," Samantha says. "Mom, Eric's doing it again."

Eric mimics his sister. "Stop making that noise!"

"He's so gross!"

Matthew shouts. "Kids! Both of you stop, right this minute."

Hope flinches, the volume of their voices jangling her already raw nerves. She closes her eyes, willing a muffling of her ears.

"But, Dad . . ."

"Eric, I said stop. Where is your Kindle? Hope, give them their Kindles. I can't take the sound of their arguing."

She doesn't hear him.

"Now, Hope."

Her eyes fly open as she jerks upright. Hope reaches into the tote bag at her feet. Gray one to Eric, purple one to Samantha. She glances at her husband's rugged profile. He is unusually quiet, and his face is unreadable. Both of his hands grip the steering wheel in a textbook ten-and-two position. Hope turns her attention to the road ahead, the gloomy dark cloud hovering above her.

Combating sounds emanate from the rear seats. Eric's video game attempts to drown out *Daniel Tiger,* and the volumes increase.

"Kids!" Matthew gripes. "Headphones."

Without prompting, Hope reaches into the tote bag and suspends the headphones toward the back seat.

When they pull onto the highway headed out of

town, only the rhythm of their tires on the pavement breaks the tense silence. Matthew's mother expects them every Sunday for lunch. Usually, the car is filled with happy chatter about Sunday School, songs the kids had learned, insights from scripture, or Pastor Robert's message. But today, the silence is deafening.

Hope turns to her passenger window and spies the clouds gathering in the blue of the heavens. As the sun slips behind them, the sky above them darkens.

"Where were you?" Matthew's voice is low, and his mirrored sunglasses are on her.

"What? What do you mean?"

He pronounces each word. "Where were you during the service?"

"I was in the ladies' room downstairs."

"The restroom? But why? Even a case of diarrhea shouldn't keep you in there that long."

"I..." Hope reaches deep down, searching for words that might explain. Words that he might understand. "Matthew, I . . . I got sick to my stomach in Sunday School, and Debbie helped me. I got lightheaded and broke out in a sweat."

Matthew jerks his head. "Are you... are you pregnant?" he whispers.

"No. No, absolutely not."

Returning his gaze to the road, he sighs. "Then what's wrong? You didn't eat breakfast this morning, but you never eat breakfast on Sundays."

Hope glances over her left shoulder. Eric, his tousled hair hanging over his forehead, and Samantha, her hair now sporting flyaways, have their headphones in place. Both are engrossed in their electronics. "I don't know what's wrong with me, Matthew." She pauses. "Mr. Hamilton and I were talking about the next study, which I have to lead, and he mentioned John Wesley and a storm at sea and then... Oh, I don't know what happened!"

Matthew's lips part.

"And I got sick to my stomach and lightheaded."

"Is it?" Matthew wets his lips. "Is it because of the dream?"

Hope drops her head.

Matthew sighs. "I suppose everyone in the Sunday School class saw you run out of the room, too."

He maneuvers the car to the shoulder, eases to a stop, and parks. Hope turns back to check on her children. Eric's wide eyes peek out from under his bangs as he removes his headphones.

"Dad?" he asks.

Matthew regards their son in the rearview mirror and speaks evenly. "Eric, this is none of your business. Put your headphones back on." Matthew waits for him to comply, then turns toward her. "Hope, this is concerning." He takes a deep breath and removes his sunglasses, passing a hand over his face. "I thought that, over time, your obsession with the accident would fade. But instead of getting better, you're getting worse. You had a breakdown this morning at church." He closes his eyes and rests both of his hands back on the steering wheel. "The rumor mill will start before we get to Mom's. Everyone will think we're having issues at home."

Hope's eyes fill. She whispers. "We *are* having issues at home."

Matthew shakes his head. "Not we, you." He gestures with two open hands. "Holding onto those old memories is breaking you." His eyebrows draw together, and frustration lines his face. "I don't know how to fix this for you. And this needs fixing. Hope, I think you need professional help."

Her breaths come fast, and tears escape her eyelids, rolling down her cheeks. With effort, she lifts her heavy head and peers through the windshield. The clouds have thickened. A numb weightiness settles over her as the sound of the first drops of rain splattering against the windshield joins the quiet hum of the car tires as Matthew returns to the road.

Tuesday mornings are Hope's favorites. For several years, she and Debbie have met in the coffee shop nearly every week, swapping stories, discussing the latest, and laughing at each other's jokes.

Hope wraps her hands around the ceramic mug and inhales the sweet aroma of caffeine and caramel. "Mmm," she murmurs. "The smell of heaven in a cup."

Debbie sits across from her at the table for two in their usual corner. "How can you smell your drink without getting frothed milk in your nose?" Debbie grins at her over her cup, enfolded in her caramel-colored, well-manicured hands. Hope would bet her right arm that the liquid in that mug is strong and straight. No sugar, no cream, no flavoring.

"How can you stand to drink that stuff straight?" Hope wipes the frothed milk away from her mouth with a paper napkin.

Tilting her head and lifting a dark eyebrow, Debbie states her go-to line. "I like my coffee the way I like my men." Hope giggles. Jesse, Debbie's husband, is indeed strong and dark. Her friend straightens and peers at her. "Say, you're looking much better than you did on Sunday morning."

Hope glances nervously around the coffee shop before she discusses Sunday's events. Nearest to them is a table of older men, whose thick Bibles are open before them. None of them attends the same church as Hope and Debbie, so she's not worried about them. Closer to the door, an unknown young woman sits alone, a book in one hand and a mug clutched in the other. The background music's volume is loud enough that even if they did know her, their voices would not be distinct.

While Debbie's mouth smiles, her eyes glimmer with concern. "You almost passed out, honey." Debbie tilts her head. "You do appear better, though. A nice Sunday meal at your mother-in-law's house may have been exactly what was called for. Lord knows you need to eat more."

"What do you mean? I eat."

"If you do, I don't know where any of the calories go. Everything I eat goes straight to my hips."

Hope scowls at her friend. "You are perfect the way you are." She didn't like it when Debbie tore herself down, even if she meant to be funny.

"So, what was that all about on Sunday?" Debbie's eyes widen. "Oh, my goodness, Hope. Are you—?"

"No, I'm not." Hope runs a finger around the top of her mug. "Funny, Matthew asked the same thing."

"Well, it's a reasonable question."

"No." Hope takes another sip. "Not possible. You have to, well, you know." Hope drops her head.

"Are you guys okay?"

Hope sighs. "Yeah, we're fine." Hope eyes Debbie's scone but has no desire to eat anything.

Debbie appears unconvinced but doesn't push the subject. She places a forkful of the scone in her mouth, chews, and swallows. "So, you're not pregnant, and you had something to eat before you came to church. Are you sleeping?"

Hope takes a deep breath. "I had a dream Saturday night. The one I have every year." Hope smooths the napkin with her empty hand. "They disrupt my sleep when I have them, and then I can't get back to sleep. Maybe that's all it was, Deb." Hope raises her eyes back to her friend. "I was exhausted."

The blaring milk frother drowns out her false bravado, and she takes in another deep, shaky breath. She leans in toward her friend. "I embarrassed Matthew on Sunday."

"What?" Debbie hisses. "Why? Because you nearly passed out in Sunday School?"

"Because I missed so much of the service." Hope again surveys the room, but no one is listening in. "Deb, he was worried about what others would think. That they would think we're not okay. I mean, exactly like you asked."

"He doesn't get it."

"No, he doesn't. He ..." Hope's eyes well up. "I've always been able to deal with this on my own. The whole thing is all so... personal. I don't want to lie on some couch and discuss my childhood."

Debbie drains her mug and sits back into her chair. "I need a refill," she announces. "How are you doing? Need another? Let me buy this round."

"No, I..."

But Debbie is already walking toward the counter.

"Okay." Hope examines the remnants of her drink swirling at the bottom of her cup. Her friend's abrupt reaction is not what she expected. The two had known each other for years. Their husbands both work for the same accounting firm in the city. She and Debbie met at the annual employee family picnic when Matthew first started there. They sat in the shade while their men played horseshoes and started chatting. Their children are about the same age and are in the same classes at school. Debbie also loves to read and enjoys some of the same music as Hope. They could talk for long periods of time. Hope believes there are very few secrets between them, and they have learned to read each other well.

And Hope wonders why Debbie had left her so abruptly. *Was it something I said?*

Her bestie returns with two fresh mugs. "The pale not-really-coffee is yours, right?

Hope smiles. "You have jokes."

"So." Debbie sits down and stares Hope down. "Are you up to it, then?"

"Up to what?"

"The John Wesley study, for Sunday School. If the timing is bad—"

"I'm fine, Deb."

"If you're not getting good sleep."

"I'm fine, really I am."

Debbie lays her right hand on Hope's forearm. "Honey. I saw you on Sunday. The very moment Mr. Hamilton mentioned the shipwreck, that's when you went pale."

Hope's friend knows only the bare essentials of what Hope's dreams remind her of yearly. Things she has attempted to keep in the past. The terror that gripped her back when she was barely a teenager and that haunts her to this day. She doesn't want to burden her friend with the depth of her fears. So, she puts on a shocked face.

"Wait! There's a shipwreck?" Hope blinks her eyes, her mouth open.

"Oh, no. Maybe not." Debbie scrunches her face. "Gosh, that was the Apostle Paul, wasn't it? I get all those guys mixed up."

Hope tilts her head and draws her eyebrows together. "Stop. You know this material better than I do."

"That would be Bob. Er, Mr. Hamilton, not me. But, honestly. Answer my question. Is studying this stuff going to be okay for you?"

"Yes, everything'll be fine. I can do it."

Debbie removes her hand. "Are you sure?"

Hope's cheeks burn as her heart races. She studies the crumbs gathered around Debbie's plate and wonders what her friend must think of her. Weak, fragile?

She takes in a ragged breath, and her voice is low and hoarse when Hope responds. "Why is everyone treating me like I'm crazy?" Hope swallows against the lump in her throat. "I'm not crazy, Deb."

Debbie's mouth drops open. "Honey, I didn't say you are." She spread out her hands. "Don't take this wrong."

"No, you just now asked me if I am"—Hope creates air quotation marks with both hands—"'up to' doing the research and writing the lessons." She has to get out of here. Her hands shaking, Hope shoves back her chair and grabs her purse. "First Matthew, and now you? Yes. Yes, I am up to doing what I need to do."

Debbie's mouth is open, questions in her eyes.

"Thanks for the coffee." Hope grips her purse strap. "I gotta go."

"Hope?" Debbie scrambles to gather her things. "Wait!"

Hope doesn't stop. Doesn't slow. She can't. She propels herself toward the entrance.

"Hope, where are you going?"

Without turning, she answers over her shoulder. "To start my research." As she passes the counter, Hope throws a "thank you" toward the barista, and then she is on the sidewalk. The door swings shut behind her.

Chapter Three

*My mother was the source from which I derived
the guiding principles of my life.*
John Wesley

Reverend John Wesley
England
Early fall, 1735

Oh Lord, thou hast searched me and known me.

The psalm of King David had run through John's mind since he awakened at four that morning.

Whither shall I go from thy spirit?

The psalm chased him the entire trip to Epworth.

At thirty-two, he should be proud of all he had accomplished. He earned a decent salary and held a prestigious position with the fellowship at Lincoln College at Oxford. Before his father's death a few months prior, John was embarrassed by his father's praise. "You've done far better than have I, John," he had wheezed. But John was unmarried. He was not burdened as the senior Samuel Wesley was, providing for a household teeming with children and servants. John could hardly compare his simpler accommodations with the relative expanse of the rectory.

Then again, he was rarely at home, but only to sleep for a few hours. His day was full of business. The chief reason he disliked travel was all the enterprise he missed. While he could, and did, get some reading done along his way, even on horseback, with each mile, time escaped him that he would never get back.

After leaving his horse and baggage at the Epworth inn, John walked down the familiar streets. He turned the corner and paused before his childhood home. He glanced at the rectory windows, toward his late father's study. His eyes grew misty as a rush of emotions filled him. Grief, of course. Grief for the loss of his father a few short months earlier, for the loss of a bygone era, of a carefree childhood. Sadness for his mother, his sisters, his brothers, and their friends. Concern, indeed, for the financial situation Reverend Samuel Wesley the elder had left for his family. And— dare he think it? —relief. Relief that he had turned down the position here in Epworth. Relief that he had not chosen the easier path. Relief, also, that he did not bear the burden of caring for them all.

Not that he didn't have a great fondness for Epworth or his family; he did. However, John was aware that serving in his hometown was not what God had called him to do.

"Mother?" John's voice echoed as he entered through the front doorway. He scanned the now sparse receiving room, his mouth open.

His sixty-six-year-old mother, Susanna Wesley, rushed into the room, reached him halfway, and embraced him. "Dear John."

He eased her out to arm's length. "Have you

moved the furniture to brother Samuel's already? The house is bare."

Mother stepped back and folded her arms across her chest. She tilted her covered head. John noted a few stray gray hairs flying uncharacteristically out around her ears. "Moved? No, of course not. Sold."

"Sold? What do you mean, sold?"

His mother jerked her head. "Follow me into the kitchen. There we can sit and talk." As she moved, she spoke over her shoulder. "You must be thirsty after hours of riding."

John followed her, relieved to find the old table and chairs intact where they had sat all his life. "I stopped at The Red Lion to secure a room and had something to relieve my thirst there. But, thank you." He settled into one of the chairs.

His mother proceeded to fetch him water, nonetheless. After she sat opposite him, her eyes bore into his. The effects of childbearing and child-rearing, along with years of dealing with a difficult and unpopular husband, were evident in every line on her face. She appeared tired, which concerned him.

"You look well," he lied. "Why have you sold off furniture, Mother?"

She sighed, but did not lower her gaze. "To settle some debts. Your brother hasn't sufficient room, anyway. I might as well be rid of the entirety."

"When will you move?"

Susanna nodded. "Soon."

"It's the least he could do."

"Son." Her brows furrowed. John noted several white hairs in those otherwise dark brows. How often he had seen the look she now gave him. He tensed. The urge to rise and flee was still a part of him, for fear she might fetch the rod. "Do not cast stones. And do not speak ill of your brother."

"It is not God's will that I move to Epworth." John studied his mother's face carefully, searching for any sign of condemnation. Seeing and hearing none, he continued, "Samuel is the eldest. Not only is it traditionally his responsibility to care for you and the girls, but scripturally as well."

"John."

He did not pursue his argument further. Mother had mentioned this when Father passed, and his brother pushed for John to assume the position in Epworth, stepping into their father's role as head of the household. Samuel, his brother, was as reluctant to leave his headmaster position as John was to leave Oxford.

"You have something you want to discuss with me." His mother folded her aged hands before her.

"I do." John leaned forward. "You remember Oglethorpe's project."

"The settlements in Georgia, in the Americas."

John nodded. "Yes. Remember how Dr. Burton talked to Father about it?"

"Yes. He is one of the trustees. Your father stated that he would devote himself wholeheartedly to that cause if he were only ten years younger." She gave a short laugh. "Imagine your father as a missionary. I can scarcely picture it. Have you heard? How many trips has Oglethorpe made since the first settlers went over?"

"He is preparing for the fifth such journey, this time with more than five hundred settlers."

Susanna raised an eyebrow. "That many. It must

be a successful enterprise if he sends that many more people after only a handful of years. I am glad that Parliament has seen fit to help the poor and indebted in our country by providing them with land and resources to make a fair, self-sustaining living."

"Yes, well." John dipped his chin.

She waited.

"Burton has been after me now for a few weeks, encouraging me to go along."

Both of her eyebrows raised, and her lips parted. "To Georgia?"

John rapped his knuckles softly on the table. "Yes." He scoured her face once again, attempting to read her thoughts, though there was no need. She always expressed them.

Whither shall I flee from thy presence? If I ascend up into Heaven, thou art there.

To John's great surprise, his mother leaned back. He had never seen his mother's back rest against any chair before.

"Tell me the details," she said. "What position are they offering you? How much will your compensation be? You will be abandoning your position at Lincoln College. What will that cost you?"

Mother had always believed that he was destined for God's greatest purposes. She was his staunchest supporter as he excelled in his studies, upheld his methodical routines and disciplines, visited prisons and hospitals, and advanced in his position at Oxford. She understood how crucial his fellowship appointment at Lincoln College was, not just for him but for his future prospects.

"That's the beauty of it, Mother," he said. "This is

a volunteer opportunity. I am set to be an unpaid volunteer missionary. And Lincoln College will hold my position."

The corners of Susanna's mouth formed a slight smile. "You are allowed a missionary sabbatical."

"I will have no obligation, no assignment."

"No compensation."

"No. But I will not need much."

"Georgia is still rough, wild country, my son, filled with hostile natives and rough, uneducated English."

"Yes, it is."

Once again, she tilted her head. "Have you agreed to go?"

"Not yet. You know me."

"You had to run it past others, those you trust."

"Yes."

"Including your mother."

John smiled. "Especially my mother."

A cloud crossed her face. "I have one concern, my son." She straightened her head, her mouth set in a straight line.

John licked his lips and placed his hands in his lap. "Yes?"

"What is your motivation?" Before he answered, she raised a finger. "You will have to board a ship, something you have yet to do in life. You hate the sea, yet you will have weeks—nay, months—on an ocean where you will not see land. You will be at the mercy of the wild elements in the New World, and not only the marshes and forests. Georgia lies strategically between British interests in South Carolina and Spanish-controlled lands directly to the south.

Therefore, you may be trapped in hostile situations with Spanish aggressors or natives concerned with the encroachment of settlers. You may get very sick and have no access to our excellent physicians. This mission could cost your life or health. And yet, you are considering it. Why?"

For thou hast possessed my reins; thou hast covered me in my mother's womb.

The urge to spring from his chair and rise to pace about the kitchen was strong. John wanted to open his mouth and tell all to his mother, to use her as a confessor. He longed to tell her the doubts in his mind, to question why he did the very things he knew he should not do, the selfish thoughts and desires that overtook him at times. What an impostor he was, merely pretending at piety, at pureness of heart, at worthiness as a priest of Christ's church.

Instead, he leaned closer to her, his eyes boring into hers. He was afraid his voice would fail him.

"I must work on my salvation, Mother." His words emerged as a harsh whisper.

This brought her forward as well, toward her son. "And this mission will accomplish that?"

He spread his arms, indicating the space around him. "There are fewer places I love to be than here. In Epworth. In this house. In your presence. This is comfort. *This* is home." He brought his hands back in front of him. "But gold is not refined by sitting comfortably before the hearth, watching the fire. It must be held *in* the fire."

Search me, O God, and know my heart; try me, and know my thoughts.

"And, Mother, if I am not fit to preach the Gospel

of Jesus Christ to the Indians of Georgia, am I fit to preach to my own countrymen?"

Susanna Wesley was not a demonstrative woman. She greeted her children with an embrace and said farewell in the same way. She might even leave a brief kiss on their cheek. But now, she grasped her son's hands in her own.

"You want my opinion."

John swallowed, nervous about her response. "Yes. Please."

Her eyes crinkled as she smiled. "Had I twenty sons, I should rejoice that they were all so employed, though I should never see them again. However." She squeezed his hands. "I know I shall see you return. I am certain of it."

Upon his return to London, John wasted no time summoning his younger brother. He was eager to share his decision with him.

Charles stepped through John's front door. "You've reached a decision, then."

John indicated a chair at his small table. "Hello, Charles, thank you for arriving so speedily. Please, have a seat."

Charles removed his coat. "Open a window, Jack. It's close and musty in here." He handed his coat to John, who hung it on a peg on the wall while his brother sat down.

John did not open a window. The air outside was far worse than that in his flat. Instead, he clasped his hands behind his back and paced in the small space before his seated brother. "Charles, you and I were destined to become priests like our father, to serve God by serving His church. We have been faithful to our call and have applied ourselves wholeheartedly as servants of the Lord. We feed the hungry, visit the sick and imprisoned, and study the scriptures to preach His word." John stopped before his brother, whose twinkling eyes followed him with amusement.

John continued. "Your ordination is in a few weeks. I have an excellent appointment at Oxford. We are on course to succeed to a degree Father never achieved."

Charles was right about the closeness of the room. The air clung to John, and sweat beaded on his forehead. But after the calm quiet of Epworth, the noisy, busy atmosphere of London stood in sharp contrast. John strongly desired his brother's full attention. He knew he wasn't telling Charles anything he didn't already know. However, he preferred to endure the stuffy heat of his loft rather than contend with the cacophony of the city on the other side of those window panes.

He grasped the back of the empty chair facing his brother. "We are both well-fed and well-clothed. We both afford comfortable, uncrowded housing."

Charles raised an eyebrow, but a mischievous smile graced his face. "I would argue against any comfort at the moment. Are you going to share your decision at any point in this discourse?"

John ignored his brother's commentary and emphasized his words, rapping his right hand on the chair back. "We are at home, whether in Oxford, London, or Epworth. We are *secure.*"

John paused, wiping sweat from his brow. He

suspected that Charles understood the point he was making. However, John had practiced this argument and felt compelled to present it his way.

"But are we, as disciples of Christ, called to be secure and comfortable? When we reflect on the ministry of Christ and his suffering, the trials of the disciples, the punishments endured by Saint Paul, the torture of the martyrs? No, they were called away from what they knew, from their homes, to preach the gospel of Christ to all the world. Why not us?"

Charles opened his mouth to respond but quickly closed it. John was approaching the end of his monologue.

"Not that I feel at all worthy of walking in the footsteps of the saints," John said. "But does not the scripture read, 'Wherefore seeing we also are compassed about with so great a cloud of witnesses, let us lay aside every weight, and the sin which doth so easily beset us, and let us run with patience the race that is set before us?' If we but step out in faith, knowing that we are not alone by following His great commission, the Holy Ghost shall go before us. Our salvation may depend on this very decision."

A door slammed somewhere below them, and muffled voices floated up to them. John sighed. A soft tapping noise interrupted his thoughts, and John looked at his brother, whose right hand had vanished under the table. The tapping was a familiar sound with a familiar rhythm.

He tilted his head at his younger brother, frowning. "You're singing in your head again, aren't you, Charles?"

"Hmm?" The corners of his brother's mouth

twitched. "You know I always have a song in my heart. The music manages to find some way out."

"Have you listened to a word I have said?"

"Of course. You've decided to go to Georgia with Oglethorpe's latest recruits."

John's jaw slackened.

Charles brought his hands into view and laid them on the table. "You spoke with Samuel." Charles lifted an index finger. "You spoke with Law and Clayton, too, as you told me you would do. What did our big brother have to say?"

John pulled the chair out from the table and sat down heavily. "He still wants me to take the Epworth rectory, of course."

"Naturally." Charles lightly tapped the fingers of his right hand on the table. "But he's not willing to take the position himself."

"No. He is not."

Charles sobered, his eyebrows furrowed, and his smirk disappeared. "What convinced you that you should go on this wild adventure?"

John tilted his head. Charles's concern took him by surprise. "You think of it so?"

Charles nodded and spread his hands. "The territory is barely cleared, Jack. The land must still be very primitive. I know Oglethorpe has placed rigid restrictions on the people, but without proper oversight, you know how people are. While the cat's away." He shrugged.

"The people need routine, spiritual guidance, and discipline. Who else but us might provide that for them? And then, to have a chance to preach Christ to the natives. Imagine it! We will encounter a people who know nothing of the cross."

Charles's face relaxed. "Ah. You visited with Mother, didn't you?"

John sputtered. "I—I, well..."

His brother laughed at him. "I expect nothing less, Jack. She has never failed to impart her wisdom to any of us. I would do the same if I were in your situation. Well," Charles scraped back his chair and stood. "I wish you the best."

John sprang to his feet. "Oh, no, Charles. You must go, too."

"What?" Charles frowned. He shook his head and held up a hand as if to halt him. "No. No, this is, this is all you."

"You *must* go." John hurried to his brother. "We are a team. We've always been a team, even before forming the Holy Club."

"Jack, I am not prepared."

I can't do this alone. John gently laid a hand on his brother's chest and let his desperation show in his eyes. "You must. We will work through our salvation, together."

A sigh of relief escaped John as Charles's face fell and his shoulders slackened. His brother sank back into his chair. His voice was gentle. "You are afraid to go alone." Charles lifted his eyes, an empathetic understanding dwelling in the depths there. "You have to cross an ocean."

"Yes, of course." John leaned toward him. "But we won't be alone."

"You hate the sea."

John squeezed his brother's shoulder. "As I've been reminded, first by Samuel, then by mother, and now by you."

Charles gave his head a slight shake. "You must be quite convicted."

John dropped to a harsh whisper as he quoted. "But let him ask in faith, nothing wavering. For he that wavereth is like a wave of the sea driven with the wind and tossed."

A sound emerged from Charles's throat that bubbled into nervous laughter. "Oh, Jack." He placed both hands on the table and pushed himself up. "As long as we're quoting scriptures, it's my turn." Sarcasm thickened his tongue. "Naomi."

John, feeling relieved, did not interrupt his brother as he spoke, agreeing with a quote from the Book of Ruth.

"Whither thou goest, I will go; and where thou lodgest, I will lodge; thy people shall be my people and thy God my God."

Chapter Four

*But as you have begun, go on in the name of the
Lord, and in the power of His might!*
John Wesley, Sermon 94

Hope
Same day

Immediately after leaving Debbie in the

coffee shop, Hope flips down the sun visor, slides the
mirror open, and stares herself down. Her round cheeks
are as red as they feel, and tears fill her blue eyes.

What is wrong with me?

She snaps the mirror closed and leans back in the
driver's seat, caught between giving herself a good cry
in the parking lot or holding back the tears and driving
away.

Hope runs a hand to smooth her light brown hair
and hangs her head. "Lord, why do I do this? Debbie's
my best friend. I know she's only concerned about me.
I know she loves me. Why did I treat her that way?"

Hope wipes her wet eyes. "I'm so stupid
sometimes." She reaches down to the cup holders
between the seats, but they are both empty. "And here I
am, thirsty, while a mostly undrunk, perfectly fine latte

sits in there." Hope grips the steering wheel with both hands and raps her forehead against it. "Stupid, stupid, stupid!"

After a few moments, she lifts her head. She's still in the parking lot of the coffee shop, sitting in her car, half worried that Debbie will exit and see her sitting there and totally embarrass her, but also half wishing Deb was in the car next to her.

Sighing, she reaches for her phone in her purse. *I should call her.* Hope scrolls to her favorites in her contacts and opens to her best friend's name. She hesitates, her finger hovering over the phone option. Then, taking the coward's way out, she taps out a text instead.

I'm sorry.

She hits send but doesn't wait for a response before texting another line.

Are you mad? You should be.

Hope pauses, noting the bubbles appear below her texts.

No, I'm not mad. Are you ok?

Okay? Pursing her lips, Hope shakes her head. Nope. She's definitely not okay.

I'm a terrible friend. I'm sorry. Love you.

Hope waits until Debbie "loves" her last text before putting her phone away. It's time to put on her big girl panties and start researching.

Despite having the world at her fingertips with the internet, Hope is old-school when it comes to researching a topic. Books are her friends, and while libraries are great, if she knows she will rely heavily on a certain resource, she'll fill it with highlights and color-coded tags. Such treatment of borrowed volumes is frowned upon, so Hope's first stop is one of her favorite haunts. Tucked away in the middle of the block in a building that's at least one hundred years old, a used bookstore holds her greatest treasures.

The vintage shopkeeper's bell dings as Hope enters, and she inhales deeply of the fragrance of the place—a musty mixture of stuffy closets, wool, and what is likely a trace of mothballs. Smiling, she nods at the man behind the counter, who barely glances up from a comic. She gravitates toward the Religion section but pauses at a table labeled "This Just In!" to thumb through the titles. Finding nothing of interest, she moves on.

Hope drifts through the stacks with low expectations of finding any references on John Wesley. She walks with her head tilted as she peruses the titles.

"Ah!" She is pleasantly surprised to find not one but six different volumes, each of which she pulls out to see how they differ. She wants them all but feels particularly drawn to a few, including a short account of the man's life that looks and smells as if it may have been stashed in a box at an estate sale and then left in a basement for decades.

Standing at the checkout with her treasures, Hope is greeted by downcast eyes. The man punches numbers slowly into a calculator, holding the page of his comic with his opposite thumb. She grins. She can't resist. "Read any good books lately?" she quips.

He doesn't so much as raise his head as he grunts a single syllable. Hope rolls her eyes. People rarely get her sense of humor. She notes a small fish tank on a stand next to the counter. Squinting and leaning in close, she searches for a fish. She spots movement by a miniature ship that is submerged on the tank floor. She inhales sharply and releases a jagged breath. She shakes her head as she mutters.

"I can't seem to escape shipwrecks these days."

Hope pulls the books from her tote bag and plunks them on the long wooden table in the center of her church's library. The sound echoes throughout the room. She heads toward the bookshelves to search for any additional titles related to the founder of the Methodist tradition.

She found three volumes in good condition at the used bookstore but was confident she might discover one or two more in their extensive church library. Wyckles may be a small Midwestern town, but her congregation was a community of readers, and the titles here had proven helpful on numerous occasions.

Hope lands upon the section in which she is sure to find a book or two on John Wesley.

"There you are," she whispers as she finds a biography. And then another. Yet another.

She takes a step back, head tilted as she reads the titles, volume after volume. *John Wesley's Complete Works*. A compilation of John Wesley's sermons. *A Plain Account of Christian Perfection.*

Perfect. Hope grins at her joke, but the smile fades as she reaches the end of one shelf and sees that the subject continues: book after book, entire volumes written by or about the man.

I should have started on this a year ago.

Hope sighs and grabs a chair from the table, spins it toward the stack, and sits, staring at the titles. The furnace fan hums, filling the room with an old-church smell.

Where to begin?

She settles on a couple of biographies bearing different titles than what she had purchased. Might as well see how they compare and what can be gleaned from each. Then she places them on the table next to her purchases and opens the books, one at a time, along with her new college-ruled notebook dedicated entirely to the subject.

The crick in her neck signals that she's been sitting at the table, jotting down notes for far too long. She stretches and stands. Best to take a potty break.

Leaving the library, she pauses at the door to the sanctuary. The afternoon sun streams through one of the stained-glass masterpieces, depicting Jesus walking on the water, arm outstretched toward a boat filled with his disciples. The sun illuminates the waves, and Hope's heart races as she focuses on the dark sea. She hurries into the ladies' restroom.

Once back in the library, the volume Hope is drawn to next is a slim one, which begins with the story of John Wesley's birth. As she reads about the style of discipline used in the Wesley household, she exclaims before reading out loud. "When they turned one year old, the children were taught to fear the rod, and to cry softly, by which means they escaped an abundance of correction." Hope laughs until tearful. "In other words, stop crying, or I'll give you something to cry about! Oh, wow!"

Clearly, the mother ran the household. So many children, all well-disciplined and educated. Hope shakes her head. *I can barely raise the two I have.*

Thinking of her children, Hope checks the time. She needs to leave to pick up the kids from school. She almost closes the little book before her eyes land on the word 'fire' on the following page.

"Wait. What?"

Parishioners had set fire to the vicarage where the family lived when John was only five. He had dragged a chest to a window and broken out the glass, the roof on fire above him.

How did he know to do that? Hope is certain that she or any other five-year-old she had ever known would have perished in their sleep.

At the precise moment the roof caved in, little John jumped from the window into the waiting arms of a rescuer. Thus, his mother called him 'the brand plucked from the burning.'

A brand plucked from the burning. That's an odd saying. Hope imagines a branding iron lying on an open fire somewhere out west, a young calf with its legs tied and held to the ground. Wincing, she closes the book and places it in the stack of volumes she has accumulated, picturing instead a five-year-old boy jumping out a window as the roof, ablaze, crashes down and sends sparks about him. Hope shakes her head in wonder. If she'd been Susanna Wesley, watching in horror as her young child stood at that window . . . She shudders at the thought. And how would the experience have been for the boy himself? To look down at his family safely outside, to feel the heat of the fire, to cough from the smoke, bits of ceiling already falling around him. Did the ground below seem terribly far away? Was he terrified? Did he cry? Or was he stoic and clear-headed until he was safe in his mother's arms?

Perhaps it was no accident that Hope was assigned this particular study subject. Though he had been much younger than her, John Wesley, too, had had a traumatic childhood.

Chapter Five

*For he that wavereth is like a wave of the sea
driven with the wind and tossed.*
James 1:6

John Wesley
Atlantic Ocean
17 January, 1736

By the third month of the sea voyage, John had ceased to be nauseated by the smells in the small, cramped hold of the *Simmonds*. Holding a handkerchief over his nose was pointless, as his handkerchiefs had all absorbed the mingled scents of human waste and vomitus.

The berths had not been built for more than snatches of sleep, and the wooden edge pressed against his thin frame. He sat hunched over, his hands gripping the edge of his bunk. The room was dark, too dark to read or write by the dim lantern light. But restlessness gnawed at him, his legs aching for the want of purpose.

"Charles?" His voice cut through the monotonous creaking of the wood and the muffled voices.

"Yes, Jack." His brother already lay in his berth above him.

"We will have the opportunity to witness to the natives in the New World."

"Mmm. Yes, perhaps."

"No, no, I believe we will. That is our purpose, isn't it? To preach the gospel to those who have never heard it? This may be the very reason we were born."

"Perhaps."

Above them, an object on the deck had rolled loose and smashed into things, lurching as the ship rocked back and forth. How could anyone rest, knowing that something was out of place and making such a racket as well?

"What did you think of the storm last evening?"

"You know what I thought of it." Charles sniffed. "I was terrified."

"Well, yes, at first, I believe we all were. 'Twas nothing as when we sailed from Cowes and passed the ragged rocks of the Needles, dangerous as that was. There, I was impressed with the majesty of God's creation."

"Quite different when a storm comes at night."

"Exactly right. And, oh, the wind!"

The wind had risen, bringing with it the anticipation of the storm to all on board, washing the ship with waves. "I was quite concerned when the sea broke over us, bursting through the windows of the cabin."

"Jack, I was there."

"I was able to eventually fall asleep, but I was uncertain I would awaken. Charles, what does that speak to my unwillingness to die?"

In the silence before his younger brother responded, a chill crept into his shoulders, shivering down his arms. He crossed his arms and rubbed them to dispel the sensation.

"What did Mother always say about that?" Charles's voice drifted down to him.

Mother. She always had something to say about everything. But, rightly so. There was never a time in his experience that she was wrong.

She wasn't the warmest human being, but that didn't mean she did not love her children. She loved them, perhaps, too much. Too much to show affection, for fear they might fall for affection in others instead of the strength of character in their spouses. She loved them too much to allow any laziness, for fear they would not learn that only hard work brings sustenance and success. She loved them too much to allow them to sin in word or deed, for fear they would lose their righteousness.

What would Mother say about my unwillingness to die? Would she be disappointed in me? Would she sympathize? Or would she see this as an opportunity for growth, an area where I can improve? What did Mother say?

"Question ourselves," John answered. "She would tell us to question our faith. To ask God for faith." He paused. "I'd be instructed to recite all of Psalm 139. 'Search me, Oh God.'"

"Jack," Charles replied, "can you believe that God would call us to preach to the uncivilized in the Americas only to have us perish at sea? What about 'the brand plucked from the burning'?"

John warmed to the memory of their mother. Although a stern disciplinarian, she exemplified motherhood for all women, providing a secure routine, a strong work ethic, a full education, and gentlemanly manners. John suspected a bias in her, however, as she had declared that he would go on to accomplish great things. And it had all started with the fire.

"The fire occurred before you were born, so, of course, you have no recollection of it."

"I've been told the story so many times that I feel as though I were there."

John ignored him. The memory was so ingrained that all he had to do was close his eyes to relive it. "I awoke to the sound and an insistent feeling. The room was so dark, dark and eerie. I started to cough. The air was thick with a black, rolling smoke." John took a deep breath now that he was able. "I heard a crackling and a wind-like roaring. I don't know what possessed me, but I jumped from my bed immediately, quite wide awake, and ran to the window. I knew enough to know I had to get out, but I was too short to climb out. There was a small chest near the window, and somehow I had to move it under the window so that I might escape. Aloft I climbed and stood at the window, gazing down at our family huddled together on the ground. I banged on the window with open palms, calling for help, but no one could hear me over the roar of the fire. The smoke was getting thicker, and the heat was intense. I felt around and grasped a thick book. I reared back and broke out the window. That got the attention of a couple of men below. They looked up at me, then one climbed on the shoulders of another and shouted for me to jump.

"And did you?"

"I did. I jumped right into his arms. And not a moment too soon, either. As soon as I was out the window, the roof collapsed. I would have perished were it not for my quick thinking."

Charles allowed only a few seconds before he replied. "So, if you had perished, maybe I'd be Mother's favorite."

Chapter Six

*And straightway the father of the child cried out,
and said with tears, Lord, I believe, help thou mine
unbelief.*
Mark 9:24

Hope
Later the same evening

"Hey, Dad, may I be excused?" Eric nearly bounces in his seat at the kitchen table.

Hope inwardly smiles at her son's respect for their houschold rules. Her husband was raised in the tradition of viewing the father as the head of the table and the home. Although her upbringing was very different, Hope had readily accepted this form of discipline.

Matthew leans over to see that Eric's plate is empty and nods. "Take your plate to the kitchen. Whose turn is it to do the dishes tonight?" He turns to Hope.

She grins and shakes her head, only once. "Not mine."

Their daughter, sitting at the opposite end of the table from her brother, sighs. "It's my turn, Dad."

"Leave your plate by the sink, Eric." Matthew

drains his tea glass. Hope notices the slurry of sugar at the bottom of the glass and sighs resignedly. She will need to pre-wash that glass before Sam has sink duty. Matthew never outgrew his childhood taste for sugar in his iced tea, yet another aspect of her husband's upbringing that differed so much from hers.

Nana hated sweet tea. She said that if God had intended for people to drink that sugary stuff, he would have made tea leaves naturally sweet.

Hope drives away memories of her grandmother. She doesn't want to feel all melancholy now.

"Dad, did you see the big tote bag of books Mom brought home?" Samantha pushes a few stray green peas around her plate. "It looks like she found a whole bunch at the bookstore."

Matthew places his glass on the table, and his eyebrows shoot upward. "You went book shopping today?"

Hope's face warms. "I started my research for the Sunday School class today. I found some good resources at the used bookstore before I went to the church library."

Matthew's mouth falls open. "Research?"

"Yes." She squints at him, her head cocked. "For the John Wesley study?"

"You're going through with the assignment?"

"Well, sure. It's my turn next to lead the class."

"I thought. . ." Matthew closes his mouth and shakes his head, as if to rid himself of whatever had entered his mind. "Never mind. Aren't there already studies on John Wesley you can get through the church?"

Hope presses her lips together and studies him.

She's unsure whether he's being impertinent or if he is genuinely concerned for her. Hope shifts her gaze toward her daughter. "You can do the dishes as soon as Dad and I are finished. Go ahead and join your brother. But no fighting."

Samantha slips her plate off the table and wordlessly tiptoes away. Hope waits until she and her husband are alone at the table, sitting across from each other. Matthew holds her gaze. "I'm sure there are plenty of such studies," she replies. "But I'm searching for the stories that will make John Wesley real to all of us."

Matthew blinks but doesn't look away from his dark eyes. "Are you going to be all right, you think?"

Hope swallows and nods her head. "I think so. Yeah."

"No more... well, you know."

"I can't promise." Hope feels her heart beating in her chest. "But I want to do the study anyway."

Matthew inhales through his nose before standing and nodding. "Good." He carries his dishes to the kitchen sink and leaves her.

She watches his retreating back, and a heavy sadness envelops her. No, she can't promise. But she will make every effort to hide her internal turmoil from him. What was that saying Nana used to say? *'Fake it 'til you make it?'* Well, she may have to do a lot of faking it to those she is closest to, especially her husband.

After cleaning out Matthew's tea slurry and neatly stacking the plates by the sink, Hope passes her family on the couch and trudges upstairs. Her black lab quietly pads behind her.

Their split-level, built in the 1960s, features four bedrooms, one of which serves as a home office. With a sigh of relief, Hope steps into her little piece of heaven, Shadow following closely behind her. The room features an L-shaped desk equipped with a home computer and a desk lamp. The far wall is lined with overflowing bookshelves, concealing its pale green paint, and the desk is positioned between twin double windows, their old Venetian blinds still intact. Several houseplants bask in the sunlight near the floral-draped curtains framing the window on the front side of the house. This room always manages to calm her.

The door latch clicks softly behind Hope as she shuts out the chatter of the television drifting toward her from the living room. She drifts to the computer desk, where her books lie open, several notebook pages already filled with her hurried notes, and sinks into the oversized task chair. Shadow settles near her feet.

All the biographies are open to the Wesley brothers' journey to the American colony of Georgia. Hope finds it intriguing that the two even considered such an enterprise. The brothers were children of a Church of England priest, raised in a scholarly home, and both became Anglican priests as well. The wilds of Georgia were far removed from their home. Only a couple of years before their trip, James Oglethorpe had brought over one hundred men, women, and children to the area in the New World to clear the land and establish a community in that untamed region. Today, the journey might be likened to a missionary expedition to the Amazon rainforest. What would have drawn them to such an adventure?

Hope was not raised in the Methodist tradition

and knew little about its founder until she married into her husband's childhood church. She had thought of the Wesley brothers mainly as the authors of hymns and lengthy sermons. However, the name Oglethorpe was familiar to her, perhaps from her U.S. history class or a movie about the Revolution. What a coincidence that James Oglethorpe was an acquaintance of the Wesley family and that he went on to establish the colony of Georgia as a mission for the poor of England while providing a buffer between English holdings in South Carolina, the French in Louisiana, and the Spanish in Florida.

None of this really explains the Wesley brothers' motivations, however. Hope crosses her arms and leans back. Was it a grief reaction to losing their father? Were they offered enough money that they couldn't refuse the opportunity? Was this fulfilling some kind of childhood dream to set off across the sea to the New World? Were they adventure seekers? Shaking her head, she grabs her pen to make a note. Though she desires to know the truth, this will make for a great discussion question.

She compares the story of the Georgia mission in each biography. There are no inconsistencies or new tidbits that provide insight into Wesley's motivation. As she peruses the volumes, Hope jots down cryptic notes: Oglethorpe, Georgia, 1732. Sailing with new settlers, 1735. 26 German Moravians.

The words suddenly blur, and Hope breaks out in a sweat. The hand gripping her pen trembles. She pauses her reading and lays down the pen before holding her head in her hands. She takes shallow breaths as her heart races. Shadow whines and sits up, laying his head on her lap. Eyes closed, she moves a hand to his smooth fur. She takes a jagged rush of air into her lungs and slowly exhales.

The office door creaks open, startling her, and Hope jolts, lifting her head.

"Hon, I'm gonna put the kids to bed now." Matthew doesn't so much as poke his head around the door.

Hope sighs with relief. She finds her voice and tries to sound normal. "Sounds good. Let me know if you need any help."

Her husband's welcome interruption halted the panic rising in her chest. However, her heart still pounds as he shuts the door. She turns back to the books laid out before her, but fears she cannot continue reading.

Storms struck John Wesley's ship in the middle of the Atlantic Ocean. Storms. Plural. Not a single storm. Multiple. As in, more than one.

Hope rises from her chair and paces, taking deep breaths—in through her nose and out through her mouth. She had read once that this kind of breathing had a calming effect. *You are okay; you can do this.*

You can do this.

She pauses before the desk. Her dog huffs at her. She resumes her pacing.

I cannot do this.

This is exactly what caused her panic at church the previous Sunday, at the moment Mr. Hamilton mentioned the storm at sea. She freaked out then, but she was surrounded by other people, and everyone was staring at her. Now, though, she is at home. She is safe. Her husband is here, in the same house. Hope shifts her attention back to the books open on the desk, her vision blurred and her heart pounding. Then she hears Debbie's voice in her head.

Are you up to it?

What is so troubling about reading and discussing something that happened nearly three hundred years ago? *Get a grip, Hope.* The Wesleys were on a huge sailing ship, not a ski boat. They were in an ocean, not a tree-lined lake. No one died in the storm or was thrown overboard.

Were they?

Hope's heart rate slows. John and Charles Wesley didn't die. That is obvious. They ministered in America and then returned to England and founded the Methodist movement. She sits at the desk, driven by her desire to know what happened next. Her hands still trembling, she skims over the next part. No one was harmed. While there was some damage to the ship, all aboard survived.

She sighs. Well, that's good. But why are the storms more than merely a footnote if there were no sequelae? Why were the events significant enough to John Wesley's story that they are mentioned in every one of the biographies? Hope shakes her head. This makes no sense to her. Why even mention the storm at sea?

Then Hope spots a simple sentence. Her lips part, and her eyes narrow in understanding. She reads the sentence out loud. "Wesley was afraid and disturbed by being afraid."

Slowly, she rereads the sentence, but this time she does so silently. Her breathing steadies.

John Wesley was terrified of the storms. He was

in the middle of the Atlantic Ocean with no land in sight, long before there was a Coast Guard or a way to radio other vessels for help. Hope takes a deep breath and then releases it. Of course, he was afraid. Who wouldn't be?

But why was he disturbed by his reactions?

Hope reads on, the question echoing in her mind. Ah. I see. While all the English on board screamed in terror, the stoic German Moravians weren't afraid. Their steadfastness shamed Wesley, causing him to question his faith.

Hope runs a hand over her face. If only she could interview John Wesley and ask him about it herself, then she would have a better understanding. But, wait. Maybe she can. Hope remembers the encyclopedia-style volumes at the church containing the complete works of Wesley. The first several volumes include his diary. Surely, he wrote about this experience in his journals. Hope glances at the clock on the wall. It's too late in the evening to run to the church, but Hope can't wait. She wants to know now.

The familiar tune of the computer startup echoes in the room. Hope opens the search engine, presses the space bar, and types 'John Wesley's journal.'

Boom. There you are, Reverend Wesley.

Chapter Seven

*I was vaulted over with water in a moment, and so
stunned that I scarce expected to lift up my head again,
till the sea should give up her dead.*
John Wesley

John Wesley
Atlantic Ocean
25 January, 1736

Although it was only four o'clock in the afternoon, the daylight had completely vanished from the skies around them. The day had darkened enough to make one wonder if it was actually four o'clock in the morning. The air carried the scent of an impending squall. However, John was ready this time. The last few storms had given him some confidence, and curiosity held him in place.

He was on deck, attempting to stay out of the way as the crew scrambled to prepare for the approaching storm. The rain fell straight down on them as they worked, strapping down and stowing away loose items. As he observed the sailors' activity, the wind strengthened, seeming to intensify the ferocity of the rain. Lightning flashed, and thunder rumbled close behind. One of the crew members rushed toward him.

"Get below deck, Mr. Wesley!"

John nodded, but as he turned, the ship pitched, and he was thrown against the stair railing. Waves crashed against them, splashing seawater over the sides and flooding the deck. Soaked, John gripped the railing, cautiously making his way down, being hurled against one wall and then the next, feeling his way into the darkness.

Perhaps this storm is worse.

Thunder shook the boat as he made his way blindly to the state cabin where he had left his younger brother. His hands trembled as they clutched at whatever stability they could find. His knees weakened, and his feet were unsteady. The crew continued shouting, their faint voices reaching his ears. John's stomach tightened, and he swallowed back a moan.

The ship will be lost. They will all perish.

"Charles!" He croaked out his brother's name, surprised by his shaky and hoarse voice. Ashamed he might seem a coward to his brother, John tried to call out again, this time with a steady, clear voice. When he opened his mouth, the ship lunged, causing his feet to slip out from under him. John fell to his knees onto the rough floor, and he cried out. Soaked through, shaking with a cold terror, he crawled forward. "Jack?"

His brother's voice was close by. Charles grasped him with both hands, helped him to his feet, and pulled him into the nearest cabin.

Thunder cracked, and more water rushed over the deck, draining through every available space into the belly of the ship. Passengers screamed as John sank to the floor.

The ship will be lost.

He huddled in a corner, pulling his knees to his chest. Charles sank down next to him.

A terrible ripping noise from above filled the air, summoning renewed screams. John briefly thought about what the rending of the curtain in the Temple must have sounded like when Christ died. That event had ushered in a new era in its finality. This tearing was surely a foreboding of their destiny.

John hugged his knees and cried.

He sat thus for what felt like hours but may have been mere minutes. Disoriented, eyes shut, he noticed the ship had settled into a much less violent rocking, and the screams had stopped. Thunder still shook him, but was less frequent now, and water had ceased rushing over them. In the relative lull, a peculiar sound reached his ears. A beautiful sound: that of human voices, soft yet clear, singing in a foreign yet familiar language.

The Germans were singing a hymn.

John dropped his head and wept anew. The Moravians were singing in the midst of a violent storm. They had no fear. They had hope. Where, oh Lord, was his faith?

John allowed the gentle rocking to sway him as he succumbed to his despair.

Chapter Eight

*They are already weary of striving (as it seems) in
vain, of labouring in the fire.*
John Wesley, Sermon 16

Hope
The following week

Wesley's journal is extensive. Fortunately, the online version features a fantastic table of contents. Hope clicks on "Wesley Sails for America." Oh, how interesting. The Wesley brothers brought along a couple of adventurous friends. She reads about how they maintained their "common way of living." She smiles, ever the Methodists. Rising at four in the morning, they each spent an hour in private prayers before gathering at five to study scripture for two hours. Breakfast was served at seven. At eight, they held public prayers. John continued studying German for the rest of the morning, while Charles wrote sermons. They reconvened at noon to share what each had accomplished since their last meeting and then dined at one.

Hope sighs. Not a single hour was wasted, from four in the morning until nine or ten at night. However, they were not yet in the open seas. She skims from

October to January, where she discovers what she seeks.

January 1736. Saturday, 17—. . . At seven in the evening they were quieted by a storm. It rose higher and higher till nine. About nine the sea broke over us from stem to stern; burst through the windows of the state cabin, where three or four of us were, and covered us all over.

Reading about this event in the man's own words, in his eighteenth-century English, makes it more bearable for Hope. Far less real.

About eleven I lay down in the great cabin and in a short time fell asleep, though very uncertain whether I should wake alive and much ashamed of my unwillingness to die.

She smiles to picture him: a skinny, diminutive young John Wesley, terrified, cowering behind a bureau in the hull of the ship. And that was only the first storm.

Their second storm at sea came six days later. That time, Wesley had stepped out of the cabin door moments before the sea broke over the side of the ship. Nothing but his pride was harmed. Hope envisions him in a black, rain-soaked cassock, his shoulder-length hair plastered to his face.

How is it that thou hast no faith?

That must have been difficult for him. After the first storm, which left him wondering whether he would survive, the crew downplayed his situation. Of course, he'd never been aboard such a vessel, and he had no idea it could become any worse.

But things could and did change, and a mere couple of days later, Hope's mouth falls open as she reads his account of their third and worst storm.

Grabbing her pen, she scribbles furiously: Sun 25 Jan journal, split mainsail, screaming English, singing Germans. She shakes her head. This is some good stuff.

In fact, this information is so good that Hope knows her Sunday School class needs to read his account for themselves. *Copy. Save. Print.*

Hope glances at the time, realizing it's much later than she anticipated. Shadow lies in the open doorway, his dark head resting on his paws. He whines when she turns his way; it's time to stop for the night. She checks on her children, her dog following her into each room. Eric is asleep, and his Kansas City Chiefs night light casts a reddish sheen over him. She wants to kiss his brown tousled hair but fears waking him.

Samantha, on the other hand, pretends to sleep. Hope can tell by the smile on her girl's face. Shadow knows, too. He pokes a cold nose at her daughter's hand, which she quickly withdraws.

Hope whispers as she leans over her. "Why are you still awake?"

With her eyes still closed, Samantha whispers in response. "I am asleep. You're sleepwalking." She gives a little giggle. "Gooooo baaaaack to behhhhhd."

Hope can't help but smile. "Verrrry funnnny. You need to sleep, Sam. You've got school in the morning."

"I know." Samantha's eyes open, and the smile disappears. Hope stands straighter. "Mom, is Daddy mad at you?"

Hope's mouth goes dry at the concern etched on her daughter's young face, and she perches on the edge of her bed. The light from the hallway pours in through the open bedroom door, emphasizing Samantha's bedspread adorned with the smiling face of her favorite cartoon—Bluey.

"Oh, honey," Hope says as she reaches for her daughter's closest hand lying on the bedspread. "No, Daddy isn't mad. I think he is only, well, frustrated. Do you understand the difference?"

"Frankie's dad got mad at her mom, and they don't live together anymore."

Hope nods. "I know, honey. But that's not going to happen in our house. Don't worry. You and Eric have a great dad. Neither one of us is going anywhere."

Hope's heart breaks as her daughter whispers. "Promise?"

Hope grabs Samantha's hand and links her fifth finger with her daughter's. "Pinky promise." Hope leans over and kisses her daughter's cheek. "Now, go to sleep. I love you."

Hope enters their bedroom and is relieved to see her husband still awake. Learning that their daughter was aware of the tension between them worries her. However, Hope has no intention of mentioning it to him. She's more eager to share her research findings with him and possibly gather some ideas for scripture passages she might include for the class. "Oh, good," she says. "You're still awake."

Matthew wears his reading glasses as he sits propped up in bed. He peers at her over the glasses while laying the book he is reading open on his bare chest. "I wanted to stay awake, in case... well." He dips his head a bit. "You know. In case you needed me." He closes the book and removes his glasses, placing them one on top of the other on the nightstand beside his side of the bed. He insists on sleeping closest to the door, regardless of where they are.

Hope smiles. "I know. I appreciate it, Matthew. I don't tell you often enough."

"So, how is the research going? Finding some good stuff for the class?"

She steps into the master bathroom and shares some of the history of Wesley's decision to go on the mission trip to Georgia as she prepares for bed. "You'll never guess who John Wesley consulted when he was making the decision to go." Hope brushes her teeth, standing in the doorway, facing Matthew.

"Um, let me guess. A Magic Eight Ball?" He pretends to hold one in his hand and puts on a terrible English accent. "What sayest thou, oh, magic ball of the eighth? Shouldest I pursue the mission to the far shore of the Americas?" He pretends to peer at the imaginary toy. "Hmph. My sources sayeth, no."

Hope spits in laughter. Finished in the bathroom, she swipes at the light switch before approaching the bed. "He spoke with several people. But the last person he consulted was his mother."

The lamp on her nightstand is turned on, so she switches off the bedroom light before slipping under the covers on her side of the bed. Shadow positions himself on the floor, as close to her side as possible, without jumping onto the bed with her.

"Ah, the great Susanna Wesley. That makes sense." Matthew leans over and gives her a quick kiss before turning off his lamp and scooting down on the bed. "Tell me more."

Hope couldn't bring herself to ruin Matthew's good mood. She resolves to shield him from their daughter's worries. Instead, she accommodates him.

"Wesley wanted to go on the trip to work on his salvation. He needed to get out of his comfort zone to grow his faith."

There is a pause before Matthew makes a comment. "He wasn't wrong."

"Apparently not. You know, if he hadn't gone on that trip, I don't know if we would be living in a Christian country right now."

"Thank God we are. So. Did you get to the..." Matthew pauses, for what she assumes is effect. "Storm at sea?"

"There was actually a series of storms. I don't think he cared much for any of them, but it was the third and most violent storm that had him so terrified."

Matthew makes an encouraging sound.

"A huge wave broke over the ship and split the main sail into bits! Matthew, all the English on board were screaming, scared out of their wits. Wesley was terrified."

She glances at her husband, who is lying on his back. The pillow kisses his dark, curly hair, and his eyes are closed.

"Meanwhile, the Moravians—there were less than thirty of them, I believe—were singing hymns. Can you imagine? It's like that one meme, you know, the one with the dog sitting at a table drinking coffee while the room is on fire." Hope lays her head on her own pillow. "Anyway, John Wesley was so confounded by the calm, peaceful attitudes of the Moravians that the next day he questioned one of their men: 'Weren't you afraid?' 'No,' the German replied, 'we are not afraid to die.' Can you believe that?" She pauses and turns her head toward her husband. "Matthew?"

He answers her with a soft snore. Sighing, Hope leans over and turns out her light.

Chapter Nine

Are your present companions angels of light?—
ministering spirits, that but now whispered, 'Sister
Spirit, come away!'
John Wesley, Sermon 121

Hope
Later that same night

Blind in the dark, Hope feels for the wall. Unsteady on her bare feet, she is thrown against a door. She heaves against the thick, heavy wooden door, which opens onto the deck. The wind whips her hair around her face. Her body is bathed with salty seawater as she stumbles forward blindly.

The cold wood beneath her feet is soaked. The ship is tossed about as if a giant hand plays with it as a child does with a toy. She lurches, feet spread wide, and flings herself forward until she reaches the main mast, her arms wrapped around its girth, grasping at ropes tied tight around it. The wind howls in her ears, and the waves crash about her.

She feels rather than hears her name called. Lightning flashes. In the split second of the burst of light, she sees a shadow before her. Thin. Dark clothing. A man with a pointed nose and a pale face. Thunder rumbles, and the roaring wind deafens her. The ship creaks, moaning as if in pain, and wood snaps. A giant tearing sound rips above her, and she raises her eyes to see the sail in tatters. Amidst the cacophony, she hears her name once more.

Hope!

Another flash of lightning illuminates the deck of the ship. The man is now closer to her. He extends a pale, slender hand.

Take my hand!

She grips the ropes ever tighter. If she lets go, she will be lost. The ship plunges to one side. The man is close now. All she has to do is stretch out her hand to grasp his. His eyes are filled with urgency. She loosens her grip to reach for him. When her hand releases the rope, a massive wall of seawater looms above her. As she lifts her chin, a scream escapes from her throat. The wall crashes down on her, and as it does, she is swept off the ship and into the dark depths of the sea.

Chapter Ten

However, there is a way to rescue ourselves, in great measure, from the ill consequences of our captivity, and our Saviour has taught us that way. It is by suffering.
John Wesley, Sermon 141

Hope
The next day

The following morning, Hope is on Debbie's stoop. The door swings wide open, and Debbie leans against it with one arm, the other poised on her hip. Her hair is secured with a bandanna, and she sports a yellow sweatshirt, black letters spelling MIZ spread across her ample chest.

"You, girl, do *not* have to knock." Then a grin spreads across her face as she opens the door wider. "Well, come on in."

"I hope I didn't catch you in the middle of anything." Hope steps through the familiar entryway as her friend closes the heavy oak door behind them.

"Actually, the dryer just buzzed and I gotta get those clothes hung up right quick before they wrinkle."

Debbie waves a hand around, indicating the living room. "Make yourself comfy, I'll be right back."

The front window faces east, allowing the morning sun to stream through and illuminate the entire room. Debbie's taste in furnishings is warm and comforting: the couches and matching loveseat are a soft leather tan, while deep burnt orange and red accent chairs complement the throw pillows. A television sits framed by shelves filled with books and DVDs along one wall. Opposite, portraits of Debbie, Jesse, and their two boys at various ages surround those of Jesse in his University of Missouri football jersey. A spinet piano rests against the wall below the picture gallery, its keys exposed and a thick music book open on the rack. Hope approaches the instrument to study the older photos she has often admired, their frames propped up on top of the piano.

A much younger Debbie stands in the center of one such picture, her arms draped around the shoulders of two other women. All three share the same amber eyes, the same dark brows, and the same wide-based nose. In another picture, the three of them surround an older, darker-skinned woman with gray and white hair, her brown eyes tinged with a sadness that hits Hope deep within her chest. No photograph of an older man, not on the piano or anywhere else that Hope had ever spied in her friend's house. Not that she expected one. Debbie has never mentioned her father, not once.

"Hey." Debbie sticks her head in the open doorway that leads to the kitchen. "Sorry about that. Let's go to the kitchen. I should have had you doctor your cup of joe while you waited."

The aroma of coffee, mingled with a lingering

hint of bacon and something sweet, swirls around her as Hope joins her friend in her bright, cozy kitchen. "Did you make your boys waffles and bacon for breakfast?"

Debbie pours Hope a partial cup and gestures toward a carton of cream and a sugar bowl. "Breakfast of Champions," Debbie quips. "Jesse appreciates it."

"You make me feel like I'm a horrible mother. My kids got dry cereal and milk this morning."

Debbie waves her hand dismissively. "I don't cook every morning."

Soft music plays in the background. Hope smiles as she recognizes the voice of her favorite Christian praise musician. Debbie leans against the counter while Hope prepares her coffee just the way she likes it. Her spoon clinks against the mug as she stirs it, turning the coffee a light tan. When she's done, she jerks her head toward the Bluetooth speaker on the counter. "Brandon sounds as great as ever."

Grinning, Debbie pushes away from the counter. "Let's sit."

The corner of the kitchen features a round table framed by large windows and white curtains that echo the teal and pink of the appliances on the counters. Four light-stained wooden chairs surround the table, which is topped with a cloth that matches the curtains. Four placemats designate each family member's place.

Debbie and Hope each pull out a chair and sit near one another, their elbows almost touching.

"Eric is sure excited about Cole's birthday party this weekend. How many eight-year-old boys are you planning on hosting that afternoon?"

Debbie laughs. "I'm crazy, I know. Cole wanted to invite all the boys in his class. I mean, that's only fair. He didn't want anyone to feel left out."

Hope's eyes widen. "Are you serious? That's what? How many kids?"

"Fifteen tops." Debbie scrunches her brows. "No, maybe sixteen, if they all show. Then he's invited his boy cousins, too. So." Debbie presses her lips together. "At max, we might have twenty boys here."

"Might as well have a Cub Scout meeting."

"Huh uh." Debbie shakes her head. "We don't need a campfire going."

"Do you need any help? I was planning to take Sam shopping to spend some quality mother-daughter time. But I'd be every bit as happy to have Matthew do something with her if you need me."

Debbie shakes her head. "Thanks, but my sister is coming, bringing her boys anyway. You spend time with Samantha."

The refrigerator's hum accompanies the background music as Hope sips from her cup.

"So." Debbie peers at Hope through her eyeglasses. "Spill it. What's going on with you? You've got something on your mind, I can tell." She gasps and places a hand over her heart. "You're not pregnant after all, are you?"

Hope laughs, waving her away with one hand. "Get behind me, Satan! Heavens, no. And Matthew and I, we're better." Hope takes a sip. "Or at least, I think we are. I don't think he's consulting a lawyer, anyway."

"Don't even joke about that."

"I know, sorry. No, I wanted to bring you up to speed about my research. For the Sunday School lessons. Because you expressed concern. Earlier."

Debbie's dark brows shoot up over the frames of

her glasses. "How *are* you doing with that?"

Hope pats her friend's arm with a free hand, reassuringly. "I think I had a breakthrough."

Streams of sunlight pour in on them as they sit, highlighting the smooth skin of Debbie's curious face as she grins with encouragement. It is as if heaven itself were present with them, while Hope prepares to open her heart to her friend. At least a little.

Hope launches in, starting with the books she had found at the used bookstore and the church library.

Debbie laughs at Hope's surprise. "A Methodist church has books on the founder of the Methodist faith... shocking. I am stunned."

Hope lightly smacks her friend's hand. "The strangest part is, my favorite is a short one, clearly written by a fan of John Wesley's. But did you know Wesley was a prolific journaler?"

Debbie pushes her glasses down to the bridge of her nose, furrows her brows, and lowers her voice. "Maybe his therapist recommended he keep a journal."

Hope strokes an imaginary beard and mimics her friend's masculine voice. "That or his freshman rhetoric professor."

"With a poster of an old mystic fellow?"

"And a really long beard?"

After they finish giggling at their use of song lyrics to mock academics, Hope sobers and fingers the handle of her coffee mug. "Anyway, the hardest thing in all of this is knowing what to leave out. There is an exhausting amount of information about the man." Hope regales her friend with stories of the fire at the priory in Epworth. After recalling how Wesley had practically saved himself, Hope shakes her head, still in awe of the resourcefulness of a mere five-year-old. "Deb, the guy must have been some kind of savant."

"Like Mozart?"

"Yeah, something like that."

"That, or Dad taught them all what to do in the case of fire."

Hope shakes her head and gulps more of her now-cooled coffee. "That would have been Mom. That Susanna Wesley was something else."

Debbie smiles. "Yeah, so I recall reading once." She peers down at her empty cup. "Do you need a refill?"

Hope rises from her seat, but Debbie lays a hand on her shoulder to force her back down. "Nope. My house. I serve you."

She sits back, easing a crick in her neck from leaning toward her friend. Hope knows she needs to open up more, discuss the feelings she has been holding in, and talk more about the accident. However, she prefers her time with Debbie to remain light and playful. She doesn't want to burden her friend with her problems, as she is quite certain that Debbie has her own share of issues that she keeps hidden.

After her friend plunks down the creamer, sugar, and Hope's spoon, more coffee flows into her cup, steam rising to greet her.

"Go on," Debbie commands. "You surely got farther than when John Wesley was five."

"Right. So, I got to the part where Jack and Chuck—"

"Jack and Chuck?"

"My nicknames for them." Hope grins over her mug. "I feel like we're best buds at this point. Anywho, as I was saying before I was so rudely interrupted."

"Whatever." Debbie's amber eyes twinkle.

"I reached the part where Jack and Chuck were sailing to America, to the colony of Georgia."

"Ah, yes." Debbie leans back in her chair. "The storm at sea that Mr. Hamilton referenced."

"Exactly. Deb, you know that's what caused my attack that Sunday, don't you?"

Debbie tightens her lips, and concern flashes in her eyes.

"It's okay. That was the cause. Anyway, I was in our home office when I reached that point. I started to sweat, and my heart got to racing."

"You had a panic attack again."

"No, that's just it. Wait, what?"

"A panic attack, like you had at church."

"That's what that was?"

"Yes. I'm well acquainted."

Hope turns in her chair to face her friend better, her mouth open. Her always put-together friend, cool, calm, and comforting, is the last person Hope would consider neurotic. "What do you mean, you are well acquainted?"

Debbie has set aside her smile, and her eyes have darkened. "Do you remember when we first met? How I used to bite my cuticles until they would bleed?"

Unbelieving, Hope regards Debbie's carefully manicured hands. "I don't remember that. I can't remember a time you haven't had these beautiful hands."

"That's why I get manicures. You think I'm gonna chew on fingernails that I spend forty dollars every two weeks to look like this?"

Hope shakes her head. "But, Deb, you're always so." She searches for what she wants to express. "Peaceful."

Her friend shrugs off the word, as if not taking possession of it. "I'm a work in progress, Hope." Her eyes pierce the air between them. "I used to have panic attacks so bad I believed I was having a heart attack. Jesse would sit and squeeze my shaking hands, murmuring reassuring things to me until my breath would even out and the moment passed." Debbie stared off over Hope's shoulder, her mouth slightly open. When she spoke, her voice dropped to a near whisper. "I had night terrors as a child." She shakes her head, as if to break away from the memories. "But then I sought help." Her eyes softened. "Have you ever seen me tap my hand with my finger?" Debbie demonstrates, gently rapping her right index finger against the side of her opposite hand, below her pinkie. "Right here on the karate chop line?"

Hope frowns, searching her memory. "Well, now that you mention it." She slowly nods her head. "I guess I thought you had a strange tic. Like how I twist my hair in my fingers sometimes."

"I learned the technique from my therapist, called tapping. Well, actually, its technical term is something else, but that's what it's commonly called. I will see if I can find my cheat sheet and copy it for you." Debbie straightens. "But here I am talking about me. You were telling me that you started to have another panic attack at home."

Hope clears her throat. She was so taken aback by her friend that she forgot where she had left off. "So, yeah. Well, when I learned that Wesley wrote about the storms in his journal, I found his account and read that version. Turns out, old English is a decent cure for panic."

A laugh escapes from Debbie. "What?"

"True story. Reading the account with his 'thou's and 'thee's makes the event so remote, it's like reading a Bible passage from a King James version."

Grinning, Debbie shakes her head. "Brilliant."

"I know I am!" Hope takes a deep breath through her nose. "Anyway, it is a fascinating story that I can't wait to share with the class."

Debbie keeps smiling, but concern lingers in her eyes. Hope tilts her head at her.

"What?"

"There's more you're not telling me."

"I said, I'll share the account with the class."

"Not his story. Something else happened. What was it?"

Sighing, Hope drops her friend's gaze. She had not intended to share the dream, not the one about being on Wesley's ship any more than her annual nightmare. Deflecting, she apologizes for her behavior the last time they had coffee together.

"Deb, I am so sorry about overreacting last time. I know you love me and know me so well. And you were right. I did have an issue doing the research. But I recovered, and I'm past that now. Can you forgive me?"

"There's nothing to forgive, Hope. I hit a nerve."

"You did, but I was rude. I reacted, instead of responding." Hope pauses. "I believe the pastor presented an entire message on that topic not long ago."

Debbie dips her head. "He sure did. Listen, I'm

very worried about you. I know you've got a thing about storms and deep water in general. But your reaction? It simply isn't healthy."

Tears well up in Hope's eyes, and she squeezes them shut to stop herself from crying. She might as well let her friend in. If she's going to cry, she should be honest. "I had a dream that night."

There is a pause before Debbie asks, "Which night?"

"The night I read Wesley's account of the storm." Hope describes the entire dream, sharing what she remembers with her friend. Her eyes stay closed until she finishes.

"That's a pretty cool dream, Hope. Wesley himself appeared to you in your dream and attempted to interact with you."

"I felt his terror, Debbie. It was so real."

Her friend clasps her hands around Hope's. She peers into Hope's swimming eyes. "Honey," she purrs, "what happened to you? How old were you when you had your accident?"

Hope cannot respond. She fights the urge to spring from her chair and rush to the door. Her bottom lip trembles. When she finally finds her voice, it comes out as a squeak. "I was thirteen."

Debbie squeezes her hands in encouragement but doesn't speak, allowing Hope all the room and time she needs to process how to express her memories in words. She presses her eyelids together, and a trickle of tears falls down her cheek. "I begged my grandparents to take me out on the boat. It was an unseasonably warm spring day. There were neighbor boys..." Hope swallows against the bile threatening to rise. "I wanted to impress them. I had developed over the winter and got my period. I was certain they would be out on their boat with their dad. Papa, he didn't think we should go. He said spring was always so unpredictable."

Hope's eyes fly open. "I didn't care. I had a new two-piece swimsuit that I could fill out. And the boys were older. They were fifteen and sixteen. One of them could drive!" Her voice caught. "Deb, I swear, I had no idea that a storm could rally that fast."

She can no longer hold back the tears, and suddenly, she is sobbing. Debbie's arms wrap around her as she murmurs reassuring words in her ear. "Hush, baby, it's okay. You let it all out. I'm right here." Debbie gently sways as she holds her.

When Hope eventually calms, she pulls away from her friend just enough to peer into her sweet face. "I'm sorry."

"Oh, honey," Debbie sighs, "this may be precisely why God put us together in the first place. Don't you worry yourself." Then her face cracks into a wide smile. "I would offer you more coffee, but maybe you would prefer a cookie and a cold glass of milk. I know that always makes *me* feel better."

Hope shifts in her seat as Debbie opens her pantry. Her friend holds aloft a package of Oreos. "Eh?"

She feels like she's eight years old but can't help nodding. When Debbie places a glass of cold milk and a plate with three Oreos in front of her, Hope is transported to her childhood. Aghast, she gapes at Debbie, who is about to commit the equivalent of a culinary felony—tearing apart the cookie and dragging the creamy center away with her teeth. Hope gasps.

"No, no, no!" she exclaims. "You dunk the entire cookie in the milk like this." Hope demonstrates, sniffling back the remnants of her crying jag, before she throws the milk-soaked cookie into her mouth.

After they destroy their cookies and down their milk, Debbie sits back in her chair and sobers. "Honey, I hate to say this, but I agree with Matthew. You need professional help."

Hope shakes her head. "I don't know. I think cookies and milk are a great alternative."

"I'm serious. My therapist has helped me a lot. How about I give you her number?"

Hope is no longer smiling. She bites her lower lip. A therapist? She then examines Debbie's beautiful nails and tries to imagine them chewed and bleeding. Maybe she is right. "I guess it wouldn't hurt to have her number."

Debbie jumps up and reaches for her cell phone on the kitchen counter. Moments later, Hope's cell phone pings. She glances at the contact who texted her and lifts her head to her friend, who offers an encouraging nod.

"Give her a call," Debbie suggests. "If you aren't happy after your initial visit, you can be as mad at me as you like."

Chapter Eleven
*Preach faith until you have it, and then because
you have it, you will preach faith.*
Peter Bohler

**John Wesley
26 January, 1736**

John waited until the following morning. He arose as usual for private prayer at four but had difficulty concentrating. The words refused to form, not even in his mind. He didn't know what his supplication should be. Well before sundown, the previous day's storm had dissipated as quickly as it had arisen. But John had fallen into a restless sleep nonetheless, even though they were gently rocked all night.

The stale air in their state cabin still reeked of fear, and John wallowed in his humiliation. Charles had not spoken about it and acted as if nothing had happened out of the ordinary. Yet John's memory of his cold, deep fear was inextinguishable, and the echoes of a German hymn haunted him.

Back in October, when he first learned that there would be some Germans aboard, John set out to learn their language. A couple of the German men also began to learn English, and John was thrilled. Three short months later, Wesley understood more than he spoke but nonetheless managed to converse in broken German.

There was one line from the hymn stuck in John's head, the memory of which tortured him the most. It was written now on his heart: *Der Herr wird seinem Volk Kraft geben.* The Lord will give His people strength.

Since the journey began, the Moravians did not remain idle. They took on chores that John's fellow countrymen believed were beneath them. John was refreshed to witness their humility and dedication to service. That morning, he found several of them tidying the common area below deck. He watched as two of the men scrubbed the floor, cleaning up spilled waste from buckets. Before long, one of them became aware of John's presence.

In broken German, John apologized. "I am sorry to interrupt your work."

The man paused and stood. "No need to apologize."

John clasped his hands behind his back. "I must ask a question, if I may."

The man set the brush aside and approached him. "Certainly, Herr Wesley. Your German is greatly improving."

John did not smile but nodded his head. He had a long way to go, but appreciated the compliment. "Yesterday, the..." Storm." The word for storm? "During the …"

In English, the Moravian suggested, "Storm?"

"Yes, how do you say it?'

"*Der Sturm.*"

"Thank you. The English were frightened near death. But you, you all, you were not afraid."

The man pressed his hands together. "I thank God, no."

John shook his head, the words from the hymn still sounding in his ears. Men, women, and children, all calmly singing a hymn from the Psalms. Psalm twenty-nine. *The Lord will give His people strength.* John spread his hands. "But were not your women and children afraid?"

"No, sir. Our women and children are not afraid to die." The man then indicated the floor. "I must continue helping my brother. Is there anything else I can answer for you?"

John closed his mouth and shook his head. When the man returned to his task, heat rose in John's cheeks. What kind of faith is this? Perhaps there was something in their simple beliefs, a lesson for him. For all his education and a lifetime spent being part of the church, when it mattered most, his conviction felt meager compared to theirs. While John was well aware that covetousness was a sin, he desired a faith like that of the Moravians.

But how to gain it?

Chapter Twelve

*And not only so, but we glory in tribulations also:
knowing that tribulation worketh patience; And
patience, experience; and experience, hope.*
Romans 5:3–4

Hope
The middle of the night, Saturday of the same week

After she tiptoes carefully out of her bedroom and down the hallway, past the children's rooms, Hope descends the stairs and heads to the kitchen. The stove clock glows the time, convicting her of not being where she should be after one o'clock in the morning.

She is unable to fall asleep.

Shadow pads up to her, his inquiring eyes wondering why his mistress is out of bed in the middle of the night. She crouches, cupping her dog's head in her hands. "Everything's okay, buddy," she whispers. "Don't worry about me."

The mug Hope reaches for in the cabinet clinks against another as she drags it out. After refilling the tea kettle, she turns on the burner and shuffles toward the refrigerator to get some milk. Uncertain whether the nausea caused her insomnia or vice versa, she grabs a spoon from the silverware drawer, dumps a heaping spoonful of sugar into her mug, and waits for the water to heat up.

John Wesley haunts her.

The whole thing is silly. This is merely a Sunday School study. Why is she allowing him to reach out from the grave nearly three hundred years later and disrupt her sleep? The dream was sufficient.

But she can't seem to escape the words from Wesley's journal. They play over in her head. She knows it isn't healthy to fixate on this specific part of his story. She read about his experience in Georgia and how he returned home to England less than two years later. As much as she wants to move on with his story, John Wesley's feelings of humiliation and failure won't let her go. His deep desire to have faith like the Moravians—one that had them singing hymns during the storms—has somehow settled into her mind. How can anyone face death without fear?

The whistle of the tea kettle interrupts her thoughts. She quickly removes it from the heat and pours the hot water over the sugar in her cup. After adding some milk, she leans against the island in the center of her kitchen.

The only light in the room glows over the sink. Hope contemplates the fixture, wrapping her hands around her mug and warming them. When she dares, she takes a cautious sip. Her mother's sure-fire recipe to calm an upset stomach has never failed Hope. She allows the drink to soothe her nausea.

I wonder what hymn the Moravians sang while Wesley and his fellow Englishmen trembled in fear. She shakes her head. *Why should she care? Is there a lesson for her in this part of Wesley's story?*

Debbie's words echo in her head again about the research. Maybe she really has bitten off more than she can chew. If Matthew became aware that the research was keeping her awake at night and encroaching on her dreams, he'd probably suggest that she give the whole thing to someone else. She could see if Mr. Hamilton would take the class over from her. Surely, there's a good six-week study out there, and she can give in and do it the easy way.

Hope peers down into her mug at the creamy concoction warming her stomach and wishes it could warm her soul. Standing in her kitchen, she is alone. At least John Wesley had his brother Charles and a couple of close companions aboard. Yet their presence hadn't been enough for him either. He still grappled with his lack of faith. *Why can't I have the faith of those singing Moravians?*

Her head shoots up as the light over the sink flickers. Is the bulb going bad? As she stares, it flickers again, then stops. Didn't Matthew change the bulb last week? Maybe he didn't screw it in all the way. Shadow whines at her feet. Hope feels a chill on her shoulders, and she shudders. The light shines steadily, the longer she stares.

Hope stands upright and empties her mug. She must get to sleep. This insomnia has her seeing things.

As she nears the sink to rinse her cup, the light flickers once more.

I will have to ask Matthew about it.

Her eyes land on the cross-shaped plaque hanging by the window above the sink. Debbie gave it to Hope as a gift. Hope reads the scripture on the plaque as if it were for the first time. "Be strong and courageous," the plaque reads. "Do not be afraid; do not be discouraged." An eagle soars between the words. "For the Lord your God will be with you wherever you go." Joshua 1:9.

Be strong and courageous. Easy for a warrior like Joshua. A lot harder for a priest like John Wesley. Or for a stay-at-home mom who is simply trying to move on from the past.

The following Sunday

"Thanks so much for meeting me a little early this morning." Hope smiles weakly at Mr. Hamilton, with Debbie at her elbow.

"No problem, Hope." Mr. Hamilton sits as he speaks, his Bible and study guide placed on the table before him in the Sunday School room. "How can I help you?"

"Well." Hope sinks into a chair opposite him, as Debbie follows her example. "I need to ask a huge favor. This John Wesley study."

"How is that coming along? Isn't his life fascinating?"

"Well, yes, sir, but—"

"Your study will make a great segue to the current study and perfect leading up to Pentecost as well, don't you think?" Mr. Hamilton pats his Bible to emphasize his words. "I know you'll do a wonderful job."

"That's just it." Hope swallows. This isn't going as planned. She intended to explain that she couldn't complete the study and plead with Mr. Hamilton to take over. "It's not going well at all. Turns out there's simply too much material, too many fascinating aspects to John Wesley. I cannot put something together in time at this point."

Mr. Hamilton frowns. "What are you saying?"

"I'm saying, well, I'm asking." Hope's heart is racing. "You know so much more about this topic than me, Mr. Hamilton. I can never do as good a job as you."

"Nonsense, Hope. You have proven yourself to be excellent at putting together your own studies. And I am running this current study." He spreads out his hands. "I can't take on your work as well as mine. I work a full-time job during the week."

Hope breaks eye contact with him. The words Mr. Hamilton uses aren't what hurts, but that he implies she doesn't have a full-time job. She may not get paid for caring for her children, but it's still work. Hope glances at Debbie, who gives her a knowing look. "Deb?"

Debbie shakes her head. "Hope, I'm already working on the lessons that follow your study." Her friend lays a hand on her arm. "Maybe there's already a good study out there. I can help you find one."

"Is there something else going on, Hope?" Mr. Hamilton leans in and lowers his voice as he asks.

Shaking her head, Hope is quick to reply. "No. Oh, no, sir."

"You had no issues at all with any of the other studies you've led. I can't help but wonder, what is different about this one?"

Her ears grew hot, and her face burned. Hope is not about to disclose to her mentor and former principal that her research has been interrupting her sleep and visiting her dreams. *Don't cry, don't cry, don't cry.* Don't show any real concern. "I can finish the study," she blurts out. "I only thought you'd be so much better at it than me."

The sounds of approaching footsteps and murmuring voices reach her ears, and Hope mumbles an apology, acquiescing. Her heart sinks in embarrassment. "I'm sorry to bring this up. Thank you for your confidence in me, sir."

Debbie stands and places a hand on her shoulder. "I need to run to the ladies' room before class starts. I'll be right back."

Hope is on her feet in a flash. "I'll join you." Turning to him, she says, "Thanks again, Mr. Hamilton. And, I'm sorry for asking you to arrive early."

The door to the ladies' room closes behind them, and Debbie checks the stalls. "Empty." She turns to Hope. "Listen, I know you think you can't do this but you can. You can. But if you want, I will help you find a study; there's still time to order copies for the class and a leader's guide. We'll be fine."

Hope hugs her friend. "You don't know how much you mean to me."

"Don't squeeze too much. I really do have to use the toilet."

Hope checks her reflection in the mirror and continues chatting while Debbie enters a stall. "I guess I can always check with Pastor Robert about prepared studies we can use." She adjusts a strand of hair. "Maybe something that avoids mentions of Wesley's childhood trauma."

"Is that why he was so afraid on the ship? He had some kind of issue with the sea or drowning when he was a kid?" Debbie flushes the toilet and exits the stall, making her way to the sink.

Hope steps back to give her access. "No, I think that was his first time on a ship."

"But the Moravians were experienced sailors? That's why they weren't afraid?"

"No, I don't think that's it. What it came down to was their faith. Live or die, they knew they belonged to God."

"But if Wesley had experienced something like that as a kid, I bet it would make the experience— What?"

Debbie's eyes meet hers in the mirror as the color drains from Hope's cheeks. Understanding washes over her friend's face. "Oh, honey, I'm sorry. That's it, isn't it? Your accident." This time, Debbie initiates the hug.

Hope clings to her friend. "Nana's death was all my fault. I was such a selfish –"

Debbie shushes her. "Forget I said anything. Splash some water on your face, and let's go make the coffee for class."

The following day

Hope moves some books aside and flips through another. Sunlight streams through the twin windows in their home office. Her notebook sits closed, with two pens resting on top, waiting. She closes the book with a sigh, then stands and walks over to the window, pulling aside the sheer curtains. The grass is growing in the unseasonably warm weather they've been having. Matthew will be mowing again soon.

Gazing at her backyard bathed in mid-morning light, Hope attempts to clear her cluttered mind. God is so good. She has her health and a wonderful family. Her husband has a great job that he enjoys. She has clothes to wear, food to eat, and a lovely house to care for. What does she have to be anxious about?

Hope turns away from the window and stares back at the books. Her failed attempt to hand off her assignment to Mr. Hamilton nags at her. He has a valid point, of course. He is leading the current study, and he works full-time. She has the time and talent to put this thing together. And while several studies are available on John Wesley, none focus on Wesley's fear of death and how he conquered it. Mr. Hamilton is right. This study serves as a perfect segue into Aldersgate Sunday and Pentecost, marking the birth of both the Methodist faith and the Church of Jesus Christ. A sort of ushering from the empty tomb of Easter to the work of Christ's believers on earth.

So, reluctantly, she returns to the task at hand. Nose to the grindstone, and all of that.

A snippet of a song from *The Sound of Music*—one of her favorite musicals—crescendos in her mind. A young novitiate, a nun-to-be, sings about having confidence in her ability to handle a new responsibility, wondering how bad it can possibly be. If only Hope shared that same confidence.

But did Maria *really* have confidence? Or was she talking herself into accepting her fate? Hope hums a few lines. Best to get to work, then. Open the books and notebook, take up the pen, and jot down more notes.

What's so fearsome about that? Mr. Hamilton has confidence in me; why don't I?

He doesn't know that something is happening at home. I'm a complete mess. I'm overreacting to this topic in an unhealthy way. I'm experiencing anxiety attacks and dreams because of all this. I need help.

Hope remembers Debbie's therapist. *Maybe I simply need to talk this over with someone unbiased, someone who can either tell me, 'Yeah, you're a hot mess' or who can reassure me that it is perfectly natural to freak out about something that happened a long time ago.*

But Hope doesn't want to dredge up the painful memories. And that's what therapists do, right? They delve into one's childhood. It's always the parents' fault.

Aside from the fact that her parents had died long before the accident, it certainly wasn't their fault. Not in her case, anyway. And it wasn't her grandparents' fault either. The blame rested solely on her. Nana wouldn't have jumped in the water to save her if she'd only worn that stupid life vest.

Perhaps she should discuss contacting the therapist with Matthew. He was the first to suggest that she needed professional help.

Hope trudges over to the computer desk and grabs her cell phone. After selecting her husband's number, she sinks into the chair and stares at the books while listening to the ringing on the other end.

"Hi, hon. What's up?" Matthew sounds surprised.

"Do you have a minute? I don't want to take time away from your work."

"This is a good time. Is one of the kids sick?"

"No, they're fine." She takes a deep breath. "I think I may need help."

There is a short pause. "You need help around the house? I mean, we can probably swing hiring a housekeeper, but you've always been so picky about how the house is kept."

Hope laughs. "No, not that kind of help." Steeling herself, Hope forges onward. "Debbie gave me the number for her therapist. She says she's really good and that I should try her out. See if she can help me with, well, you know. You said yourself that I should get professional help." There was silence. "Matthew, are you there?"

"I'm still here."

"Of course, I don't want to. All therapists want to talk about is one's childhood, right? I don't know that I can bear dragging up old, painful memories. But maybe it will help? Debbie says what I had was a panic attack. All I know is that the experience was awful, and I don't want to feel that again. And then, of course, there are the dreams. So. What do you think?"

Hope chews the end of the pen she grabbed from the desk. She tries to picture her husband's face right now. She hears him take a deep breath before he speaks.

"I think it's a wonderful idea. If you're leaning toward making an appointment, I agree. I don't know if our insurance will cover the service, but I don't care." Hope hears him exhale. "I'm proud of you, you know."

Her face flushes, and she catches her breath. "What? Why?"

"For realizing you're struggling and wanting to do something about it. No more sweeping everything under the rug, so to speak. This is a huge step."

"So, it's okay for me to call? Make an appointment?"

"Yes, of course. I hope you can get in soon."

After they disconnect, Hope runs a finger over the small John Wesley biography. As frightening as it is—the idea of confiding in a complete stranger about personal issues and inviting someone into her inner circle—she can't keep running from her past and the issues tied to it. Perhaps it's less about her faith in God and more about her faith in herself. John Wesley consulted others. So why not her?

She retrieves her cellphone, locates the contact Debbie texted her, and hits "call." After only two rings, a woman's voice answers.

"Yes, ma'am," Hope says. "If you are taking new clients, may I make an appointment?"

Chapter Thirteen

*Behold, thou desirest truth in the inward parts:
and in the hidden part thou shalt make me to know
wisdom.*
Psalm 51:6

Hope
Later, the same day

In the early afternoon, after a light lunch and tidying up the kitchen, Hope returns to her research. The phone call to the therapist strengthened her resolve to continue her assignment.

She feels compelled to find scriptures about fear, so Hope opens the electronic copy of the Bible on her cell phone and searches for the word 'fear.' She grimaces as she notes the high number. Remembering the plaque in her kitchen, Hope decides to change her search to 'afraid' and scans through the results for the phrase 'do not be afraid.' There are still many scriptures containing the command, but she is struck by how many times God tells Joshua not to fear. The Psalms provide similar encouragement. The Old Testament prophets weren't all doom and gloom, as she notes down passage after passage urging the people of God to have no fear. And why? Because the LORD is with them.

Daniel, chapter ten, verse nineteen captures her attention, and Hope's lips part, her bottom lip trembling. She reads the words aloud.

"Do not be afraid, you who are highly esteemed." Hope wets her lips. "Peace! Be strong now, be strong."

She lays down her cell phone. Do not be afraid. Be strong. Hope covers her mouth with her hand as warmth fills her chest. So many of God's people needed to hear those words. She needs to hear them too. Do not be afraid. At what point might John Wesley have heard those same words?

Hope turns to the biographies, with all the volumes now laid open to the next chapter in the Wesley brothers' lives. No wonder one of the books refers to the Georgia chapter of Wesley's life as "the American Fiasco." The brothers had high expectations, but nothing turned out as they were told. Charles was appointed secretary to Governor Oglethorpe. However, after being set up by a vicious pair of women and made to look bad in the eyes of the community, Charles resigned and returned to England alone after just a year and a half. John remained, determined to serve his pastorate. Nevertheless, his strict methods and uncompromising standards did not sit well with his parishioners.

Hope giggles as she reads about attracting the attention of young, marriageable ladies. John Wesley was charmed by the eighteen-year-old niece of the magistrate of Savannah, Georgia. However, he couldn't decide regarding her, asking his friends and trusted advisers whether he should court the young woman. Apparently, he waited too long to make his move, and the young lady made the decision for him by becoming engaged to another and abandoning her religious practices.

"Well, Mr. Wesley," Hope laughs. "It seems you should have left well enough alone." Though John felt somewhat relieved, his feelings were hurt, and he publicly rebuked the young lady for straying from the faith. He even became embroiled in a lawsuit over the whole incident. Apparently, one does not create a scene with the niece of the local justice of the peace.

"Oh, my word!" Hope's voice echoes in the room, reaching the part about Wesley's sudden, unannounced departure from Georgia to sail back to England. "You committed an Irish goodbye!"

Reading Wesley's journal, it becomes evident that the lawsuit was fabricated to force him to leave, with his departure as the ultimate goal. That poor man, to realize he was unwelcome. Surely everyone has, at some point, felt that kind of pressure. There likely wasn't much in Wesley's past that had equipped him for that level of ugliness.

But, of course, there was the fire at age five. The very same people assigned to his father, their neighbors, were the ones who burned the house. John Wesley likely grew up understanding how terrible people can be to one another.

The afternoon sun reflects through the windows, casting a soft glow in the room. Hope leans back in the chair and rubs her eyes. She is so engrossed in Wesley's story that she has failed to take notes. She reaches for the pen and notebook, jotting down a few lines that she might use for the lesson. Pausing, she then writes a question: When have you experienced false witness against you?

After reviewing her notes, she refocuses on Wesley's relationship with the Moravians, the group of German believers who had greatly impressed him. He had maintained connections with them while in Georgia, but Peter Bohler was the most influential figure on Wesley. Feeling depressed after the misadventure in Georgia, in a state of complete defeat, he recalled how he had been questioned once off the ship in Georgia about whether he had a personal relationship with Christ. Wesley had given a vague negative response, which must have weighed heavily on him as he doubted whether he should even continue his priesthood after his self-perceived failure. It was Peter Bohler who advised him to preach faith until he discovered it, and then, because he had found it, to preach faith.

Hope smiles. "I'm glad you didn't quit the ministry, Reverend Wesley."

She reached the part in the story where Charles Wesley was, for a second time, reported to be on his deathbed. He then gladly told John that he "believed."

Oh, man, that must have hurt. Here, John Wesley had prayed fervently for weeks, months even, for faith, and his little brother experienced the reality of the Holy Spirit before he had! Hope shakes her head and jots down more notes. She writes the words reportedly asked of John Wesley. *Do you know Jesus Christ? Do you know that He has saved you?*

The front door opens and then slams shut, startling her. The excited voices of her children prompt her to check the time.

"Oh, no! I should have started on dinner by now!" Hope bolts from the desk, leaving her books open, and hurries downstairs.

A couple of weeks later

"It's very nice to meet you." Hope's voice is a bit squeaky. With sweaty palms, she shakes the therapist's hand before following her into a cozy room off the lobby. She had arrived thirty minutes early, sitting in her car in the parking lot, thinking of any number of excuses to avoid going in. Maybe she could call the therapist and tell her she had car trouble (she hadn't) or that one of the kids got sick at school (they didn't). She had to perform some out-loud cheerleading to herself to get out of the car and walk into the lobby.

Hope sits on the edge of an empty chair and surveys the room. The walls are sparsely decorated, while the furniture is modern and comfortable. There is another chair beside her, and a coffee table stands between her and the chair occupied by the therapist. While the blinds are closed on the only window, sunlight peeks around its corners, adding a warm, natural light to what the floor lamps provide.

"Is it all right if I call you 'Hope?'" The therapist sits comfortably with a legal pad on her lap and a pencil in her hand. Her eyes radiate a warm bronze, and her curly red hair is neatly tucked behind her ears. Not at all intimidating.

"Yes, of course." Hope gives a little laugh. "Since that's my name."

You may call me Rachel. Thank you for completing your forms ahead of time. It gives us more time to talk and get to know each other better.

"Of course." Hope is relieved that the background music in the small waiting area isn't playing in this room. She finds that too distracting in other places.

Hope feels jittery inside. She blurts out, "What? No couch?"

Rachel offers a polite laugh. "No, I was careful to avoid that old cliché. Get comfortable, Hope. You seem ready to jump up and run for the door."

Hope's smile fades, realizing that she is indeed perched near the edge of the chair. She scoots back on her seat and straightens her shoulders. "Sorry."

"No worries. Do you need some water or some tea?"

"Not for me, thanks." Come to think of it, her throat feels a little dry, but Hope prefers to move on to the hard stuff.

"Now, before we begin, do you have any questions for me, any concerns you may have?"

Hope notices the box of tissues on the coffee table. There's a similar box on the end table to her right and yet another on the matching table to the left of the empty seat beside her. "Looks like I am expected to cry a lot."

This makes Rachel smile. "Not expected, but yes, it happens a lot in here. I know you're nervous, but you have nothing to fear here, alright?"

Easy for her to say. But Hope remembers that this woman is a professional. She nods her head.

"Now, Hope, I know you've already answered this on your forms, but please, tell me why you are here today."

Hope clasps her hands and studies them resting on her lap. "I have recurring dreams. Well, nightmares, really. They've become pretty disruptive to my sleep. Then I get emotional easily, especially when I'm tired. And recently, I've done some research for our Sunday School class and have experienced some physical reactions that I don't think are, well, normal. I think it's all probably related. My husband was eager for me to seek counseling, and when Debbie gave me your contact information, I took that as a sign that I should reach out."

There is an awkward silence. A clock ticks off the seconds.

"Hope?"

She raises her head. "Yes?"

"What kind of physical symptoms have you been experiencing? Can you describe them for me?"

Hope nods. "Sure. Well, my stomach feels weird, a kind of sick feeling. Sometimes it gets worse, and I'll have nausea. I even vomited one time. I get shaky—my hands and inside, and I guess everywhere, like shivering. I'll get all cold inside. Not on the outside so much." Her voice tapers off.

Rachel waits a moment. "Any chest tightness or shortness of breath?"

"Sometimes, especially shortness of breath. Sometimes my heart races."

"How long do these episodes last?"

"It seems like hours sometimes, but I guess maybe five, ten minutes? Sometimes longer. If an episode happens from the dream, it can take me quite a while to get settled and back to sleep."

"And you say that doing research has brought on these symptoms? Is it anticipating having to do the research?"

Hope shakes her head. "No. I enjoy doing research. There's a part of the story I'm researching that bothers me. About a storm at sea."

The therapist jots down some notes and checks the forms before she returns to meet Hope's gaze. "And the recurring dreams. Do you think the issues with this particular research are associated with the dreams?"

"Yes. The dream is nearly always the same." Hope halts. After meeting this woman, she didn't want to dive into this topic so quickly. But digging deeper is why she is here, isn't it? "I was in a boating accident at age thirteen and almost drowned. Whenever the anniversary date nears, the nightmares tend to return. I mean, sometimes, I have them at other times of the year, but not as predictably."

"Can you tell me the dream?"

Hope shook her head. "I'd rather not. I mean, not yet. I'm not really comfortable."

"It's okay, Hope. Only share what you feel you can. Why do you think the nightmare occurs around the anniversary date?"

"I dream of the accident."

"I see. Some of the same components, or an actual replaying of the accident, would you say?"

"A replaying."

"I see." More scribbling. "And the research is about a storm at sea. Was there a storm at the time of your accident?"

Hope nods. Her upper lip is sweaty, but she hesitates to wipe it away. She wants to avoid drawing Rachel's attention to it.

"And how is your sleep? I mean, usually."

"If I have no nightmares, I sleep pretty well."

"You share a bed?'

"With my husband, yes."

"And he sleeps alright?"

"Like a baby. Doesn't even really snore."

"Okay. Is there anything else that seems to trigger these feelings you get?"

Hope wipes her hands on her pants. "I avoid things that might."

"Such as?"

"Boats. Bodies of water. Pools." She pauses. "I'm not fond of thunderstorms either."

Rachel takes note of this and then locks eyes with Hope. "Would you like to know what I think may be happening with you?"

"Please."

Rachel taps the pointed end of her pencil on the legal pad. Hope notes that the eraser end displays teeth marks. Interesting.

"My working diagnosis is PTSD or post-traumatic stress disorder, with subsequent death anxiety."

Hope frowns. "Death anxiety? But I'm not afraid of death, per se. I'm afraid of water."

"Your fear of water is actually a fear of death, Hope. What do you think the water will do?"

Hope found herself again on the edge of her chair seat. "I'm afraid of drowning."

"Okay, and what would happen if you drowned?"

"Oh, my goodness." This was a new concept for

her.

The therapist nods. "There is a proven treatment for this, called Cognitive Behavioral Therapy. CBT. Are you familiar with it?"

Hope shakes her head. "No."

"The therapy has more to do with changing how you think about things and how to respond to them in positive ways instead of negative ways. How does that sound?"

"That sounds good if that's what you think will help me."

"Absolutely. Alright, I have some homework for you. I'd like you to keep a journal. I have one for you if you'd like. I want you to write down the thoughts, beliefs, emotions, and images that come to mind about your problem. Then, I want you to write down the physical responses, how you feel, how you act, and your behavior in reaction to these thoughts. After that, we will gain more insight into what goals to set for the therapy. Make sense?"

Hope accepts the journal but can't help thinking of Wesley. When she opens it, she sees the assignment printed on the first page. "Thank you."

"You're welcome, Hope. How are you feeling right now?"

"Fine. I mean, I feel a little overwhelmed, but it will be good. When should I return?"

"Let's make an appointment for next week."

Hope nods and offers a weak smile as she rises. She clutches the journal in her left hand while extending her right hand. "I'll see you next week."

Chapter Fourteen

*Justifying faith implies not only a divine evidence
or conviction that "God was in Christ"... but a sure
trust and confidence that Christ died for "my" sins,
that he loved "me," and gave himself for "me."*
John Wesley, Sermon 5

John Wesley
London, England
24 May, 1738

Though the weather was pleasant enough for late May, a chill crept around John's shoulders. As he walked briskly, the early evening sun angled away from him, prompting him to adjust his cloak. His stomach grumbled. Had he eaten today? He thought back. Yes, he had eaten a bit in the morning. That should have been sufficient.

The last thing he wanted to do was attend the society meeting that evening. As little as he relished the idea of listening to someone less educated than himself drone on, he was even less enthusiastic about hearing this particular person lecture on Martin Luther's commentary about Saint Paul's letter to the Romans.

John sighed.

He should instead be visiting with Peter Bohler again. However, his last encounter with Bohler had left him feeling depressed. After visiting with his brother Charles—Charles, who John had been told was once again on his deathbed—he had hurried to visit, only to find his younger brother fully recovered and babbling on about being converted! Like him, Charles was a reasonable man. Perhaps it was all a side effect of the fever. Surely, Charles had been hallucinating. The Holy Ghost has not visited Earth since the destruction of the Temple in Jerusalem in 70 AD.

But Charles was so convinced that he and Bohler had prayed for John to also receive the Holy Ghost. Peter then met with John separately, teaching him more about the ways of the Moravians. The Moravians had a calm, settled peace and a personal relationship with God. John's father had never taught about a personal relationship. In fact, none of John's training and service to the Anglican Church had ever emphasized a personal relationship. Theirs was a corporate salvation. The Church was the body of Christ, and the Church was saved. One was saved by adhering to the teachings of the Church, which were, in turn, the teachings of Christ. I visit the imprisoned, feed and clothe the poor. I tithe, read, and study scripture. But never—not once—had John experienced the holy presence of God, as Peter and now Charles claim to have experienced.

Hoofbeats and the clacking of carriage wheels echoed behind him, and John stopped, allowing them to pass. He was nearing the house on Aldersgate Street where the meeting was to take place. Although he was this close, he felt tempted to turn around and return home. There, he could read Luther's preface to the

Epistle to the Romans himself. Better yet, he could re-read Saint Paul's entire letter. In its original Greek. That might take up the whole evening. Yet, each hesitant step nonetheless brought John closer and closer.

He arrived at the meeting place and paused in the street, staring at the house. His acquaintances were inside, waiting for him. He should feel eager to see them. Yet, John crossed his arms, his eyes locked on the house, feeling very much alone.

It wasn't too late. He could still turn around and go back home. Back to his cozy sitting room. Back to his books. Or he could stop at an inn to grab a bite to eat first.

The front door swung open. The homeowner signaled for John to come in, and then there was no turning back.

Half an hour later, as he sat on an uncomfortable straight-back chair, only half-listening to the man, he drifted back to earlier that same morning. The New Testament reading was from the Second Letter of Saint Peter. Whereby are given unto us exceeding great and precious promises, that by these ye might be partakers of the divine nature. Knowledge of Christ promises to make us partakers of the divine nature. In Romans, Saint Paul wrote that, through Christ, we have access to God's grace. In other words, faith in Christ, faith alone, does more than simply pave the way to heaven; it provides us with hope. Saint Paul was not inferring a collective salvation—that only through the church is one saved—or that only by our works and best efforts is one saved. Rather, it is by our faith—my faith!—that we are justified before God.

Oh, Lord, I believe! Help my unbelief!

John began listening to the speaker. Although he had sat still for some time, he found himself quite interested and much more alert. He slid to the edge of his seat, leaning forward. The man began describing the change that God can work in one's heart. A warmth, both unique and strangely familiar, emanated from within John. There was a calming presence, stilling his internal doubts and fears. It was a kind of peace he had never experienced before, as he was filled with a deep knowledge that Christ's salvation was for him, John Wesley. He was not alone, for John was convinced the Holy Ghost himself was with him.

The Holy Ghost himself.

In slow motion, John stood. The man continued speaking, but John no longer heard the utterance. Wesley opened his mouth, and with a loud voice, he said, "Praise be to the Lord our God, and worthy is the lamb that was slain!"

The speaker stopped mid-sentence. John's friends spun around in their chairs to stare at him, their mouths dropping open at his interruption.

"My friends, my friends!" John exclaimed. "I am filled with the love of Christ!" He turned to his companion on his right, who rose from his seat, eyes wide. "Richard, my friend. Christ died for you. He is risen for you!" John pointed a finger at Richard's chest. "And for me. For me!" Wesley indicated with an extended arm at the others in the room, who still gaped open-mouthed. "For all of us!"

John couldn't help himself. A surge of energy swept over him with a sudden sense of urgency. He knew precisely what he had to do.

"My friends," John finally said, "I would stay with you to share further in this blessed experience with you, but please excuse me. I must go see my brother, Charles."

With that, John Wesley hurried to the door and nearly sprinted down the street.

Chapter Fifteen

*Now faith is the substance of things hoped for, the
evidence of things not seen.*
Hebrews 11:1

Hope
A couple of days after the therapist appointment

When Debbie called her yesterday to ask if
Hope wanted to drive with her to Glade Top Trail,
Hope jumped at the chance. Time with her bestie? You
better believe it.

Hope glances at Debbie, who is sporting a black
ball cap. Debbie's sunglasses hide her eyes as she peers
at the road, the sun visor lowered. Her left hand is
splayed across the steering wheel, while her right hand
holds her to-go cup.

"I stopped and got you your latte." Debbie adopts
a haughty accent as she pronounces the last word,
waving toward the cup holder.

"Gee, thanks." Hope grabs the coffee and takes a
sip. "Ah, that's perfect." She shifts her attention to the
road ahead. "I don't know that I've ever been to Glade
Top. What is it?"

Debbie laughs. "You agreed to go, but didn't

know where? You're funny, girl."

Hope shrugs. "You offer to get me out of the house so we can spend some time together on your day off? I don't care where we're going."

Debbie clears her throat and puts on her best public radio broadcasting voice. "Glade Top Trail is a national scenic byway, with panoramic views of the Mark Twain National Forest."

"Ooh, fascinating!" Hope takes another sip. "Do I have to walk trails?"

"Nah." The dark, tight curls flying out from under Debbie's ball cap shake with her head. "I only wanted to go for a drive. It is promised to be a pretty spring day, and the mountain calls to me." Debbie's eyes cut away from the windshield to Hope. "Yeah, with what you're wearing, we're not going to be taking any walks through the weeds."

Hope peers down at what she calls her 'hippie dress,' multi-colored, flowing, and mid-calf length. "This old thing?" She had thrown on a pair of flat sandals with brown double straps and bronze buckles.

"All you need to top off that outfit, darling, is a floppy, wide-brimmed hat."

Grinning, Hope replies, "Oh, I have one of those at home, and yes, I almost brought it." She points to the trees lining the road on her side of the two-lane highway. "Appears a little windy today. The floppy hat might well have flown off my head."

"Mmm. Oh, hey." Debbie presses the volume button on her steering wheel to raise the music. "That voice. A heavenly voice to sing heavenly music."

Hope and Debbie sing along. As they sing the title line, Debbie throws both hands off the steering wheel and raises them into the air. "Come out of that grave!"

"Deb!" Hope reaches toward the wheel, but her friend chuckles as she recovers it herself.

They listen to the end of the song, and then Hope reaches to turn the volume back down to a background level. "I had my first therapy session a couple of days ago."

Debbie jerks her head toward Hope. "Really? So, tell me about it. Do you like her?"

"Rachel was amazing, really. I don't know what I expected, but it wasn't that. She went out of her way to make me feel comfortable and safe."

"Ah, honey, that's great." As they round a curve, the sunlight glares directly at them, and Debbie swipes the sun visor down. "She's done wonders for me. I'm glad that you two hit it off."

"Well, it was only the first session. But yes, I think it may work out well. I have homework."

Debbie bobs her head. "Yep, that sounds like her."

Hope provides Debbie with an account of the therapist's diagnoses and treatment plan. "Have you heard of CBT?"

"Cognitive Behavioral Therapy. Yes, ma'am, I have."

"My homework involves identifying my thoughts and beliefs about my problem." Hope leans back against the car seat, stretching her neck and closing her eyes. The sunlight warms her face as she allows herself to drift back to the appointment with Rachel and how Hope had been initially apprehensive, uncertain about what to expect. She feels optimistic about the therapy now, believing it could change many things for her.

"I used to be a really great swimmer," Hope murmurs.

Debbie provides empty space in their conversation for Hope to fill, keeping her eyes fixed on the road ahead and offering only an occasional encouraging sound in her throat.

"The dreams I have are basically a replay of the boating accident. I was sunbathing in my new swimsuit on the front of the ski boat. Papa had the kind where the windshield hinges in the middle, and it had seats up front where I could stretch out."

Hope lowers her head and turns it toward her friend. "Why are we so stupid as kids?" A slight tremble in her voice surfaces unexpectedly.

Debbie snorts. "Don't you remember that comedian who did entire skits based on the idea that children are brain-dead?" She reaches her right hand over to pat Hope on the knee. "All of us were dumb when we were kids, honey. Don't feel alone."

Hope's voice caught in her throat. "But Papa had said it might storm. And although it started out as pretty and warm as it is today, just like that." Hope snaps her fingers. "Dark clouds gathered, seemingly out of nowhere. It got dark, and the wind picked up."

Bowing her head, Hope lowers her eyelids, fighting the wave of panic as her heart races and her chest tightens. Her breathing quickens as the car slows and eases to the shoulder.

"Hope." Debbie's soft voice reaches her as if from a distance. "Look at me." Debbie's warm hand clamps onto Hope's clammy one. "Breathe."

Hope obeys.

"That's right. Lift your head, open your eyes.

Look at me and breathe. You're in the car with me. Take a deep breath in." Debbie demonstrates. "And exhale. Good. One more deep breath in."

Hope's heart slows, and the stranglehold around her chest eases.

"And exhale." Debbie still grips Hope's hand and waits. The car sways as another vehicle zooms past.

"You feel that, Deb?" Hope's voice was small as if she had shrunk to child-size. "That rocking? That's merely from a car going by. Imagine how a boat can rock on stormy water." Hope takes another deep breath. "That's all it took. A gust of wind on a choppy lake."

Hope removes her hand from Debbie's to wipe at her wet cheeks. "In an instant, my entire life changed."

Debbie watches her through her sunglasses, waiting until Hope waves a hand. "I'm okay. Thanks. Let's keep going."

"You sure?"

Hope nods. "I gotta see this awesome scenic highway."

"Byway."

Hope sniffs. "Whatever."

Cautiously, Debbie reenters the roadway, the soft music filling the car. It isn't long before she activates the blinker and steers the car to the right onto a gravel road. Hope breaks the silence. "Wow, Deb. I had no idea this was even here."

Clutching the steering wheel with both hands, Debbie creeps along the rough road and offers Hope a broad, toothy grin. "Wait 'til we get to one of the lookouts. You are gonna love it."

After several stops, during each of which the friends jump out of the car with their cell phones to capture breathtaking views of the early greenery—leaves erupting from oak trees and redbuds in full bloom—Debbie turns into a gravel parking lot at a picnic area. Hope turns to her, and her mouth drops open. "Picnic?"

Debbie whips off her sunglasses with a flourish and wags her eyebrows at her. "Hey, Boo-Boo, I brought along a pick-a-nick basket." She does a great Yogi Bear impression.

"Okay, Yogi." Hope plays along. "Let's have a bite to eat."

After devouring the sandwiches and chips Debbie had packed, they sit on a low bench, sipping water from plastic bottles. They are perched atop a glade, a thin-soiled area that exposes bedrock and is scattered with bushy green stems.

"Is this what the old folks call a bald knob?" Hope asks.

"Yeah, it is. Doesn't appear anything like those zany shows in Branson, huh?"

Hope chuckles. "Not at all. I guess they call it 'bald' because there aren't a lot of trees on it. But it's hardly sparse in vegetation. Check out all the herbs growing around the rocks."

"We'll have to return in the summer when the wildflowers are blooming."

Hope takes a deep breath, inhaling the fresh scent of spring. On a late April day in the middle of the week, there was very little traffic. "What a perfect day to be here, Deb. Thanks for bringing me."

Debbie takes a swig from her water bottle, then screws the cap back on. "You're welcome, Hope. I needed this today."

Hope tilts her head toward her friend, who gazes out across the glade at the rolling Ozark hills. She secures a strand of her blonde hair that has whipped across her face as a gust of wind hits them. She doesn't interrupt the pause in their chatter as she turns back to take in the scenery. As they sit in comfortable silence, the brilliant sun dims. Hope glances up at it as a few gray clouds skitter across the sky. Of course. The only dark clouds in the entire Ozarks have to threaten their beautiful day in nature.

"Hope." Debbie's voice breaks the spell. "You've been so brave, opening up to me about the accident, especially when talking about it is so troubling for you."

Hope doesn't respond immediately. She and Debbie continue to gaze at the beauty before them. "You're my friend. If I am to tell my therapist about the accident, I should feel free to talk to you about it first."

Debbie makes a *tsk* sound and takes a deep breath. "But that's it. I haven't trusted you with my ugly childhood. I never wanted to dampen the mood between us. I want our friendship to be a light and fun place to hang out. Besides, I've worked through it with Rachel and, of course, with Jesse. I guess." Debbie turns at her waist to face Hope. "I guess I should be more open with you."

Ugly childhood. Hope remembers the picture in her friend's house, of Debbie, her two sisters, and their mother. The absence of any pictures of anyone who could be Debbie's dad. She peers down at Debbie's manicured hands and remembers her friend discussing how she used to chew those nails and cuticles. Hope comes to the realization that her friend wants to share painful memories. But if she notes Debbie's tapping, Hope vows to herself to stop her.

"Deb," Hope ventures, "only share what you want with me. You owe me nothing. But I will listen with a heart full of love for you. Okay?"

The corners of Debbie's mouth twitch before she straightens her torso and resumes her watch over the glade and its surrounding hills. She opens her mouth and tells Hope a story, as foreign to Hope as if she had begun with 'once upon a time.' Debbie reveals that her paternal lineage, along with that of her half-sisters, is unknown to them. The man who married their mother was not their father and, unfortunately, begrudged their existence. Debbie does not delve into sordid details but shares enough that Hope feels compelled to hunt down the man and make him pay for what he did to Debbie just before she began to blossom into womanhood.

They sit in silence for several minutes, acknowledging the dark energy of Debbie's stepfather. Hope finally finds her voice. "Did your mom know?"

Debbie shakes her head. "Not until he tired of me and was about to go after my sister. That's when she found out." Debbie takes a shaky breath. "I thought she was going to kill him. I believed he was a dead man."

Debbie turns her amber eyes to Hope, who sees a haunted hurt there. "Much as I hated him, I knew Mama would get caught and me and my sisters would get torn apart, put in foster care." She shook her head. "So, I begged her."

Hope sniffs, her nose runny from the withheld tears. It was her turn to place a hand on that of her friend. Debbie draws in a stuttering breath. "He left. We never heard from him again." She scoffs. "I can only imagine what Mama threatened him with."

Hope slowly shakes her head and parts her lips, searching for the right words. As if reading her mind, Debbie cuts her off abruptly.

"You don't have to say anything, Hope. I appreciate you being here." She gestures toward the valley before them with her other hand. "To share this with me. For being my friend."

The dark clouds have disappeared, as if Hope had imagined them. The sun was sloping away from the mid-sky. Debbie slapped her thighs in resignation. "I guess it's time we headed back. I want to get supper started before the boys get home from school." Debbie angles her head at Hope. "You ready?"

"Yeah, I suppose."

Back in Debbie's car, when her friend is about to put the car into gear, Hope is struck by a thought. "You know what? I think God meant for Jesse and Matthew to work together. So that we would become friends."

With her sunglasses back in place and hands on the steering wheel, Debbie throws a lopsided grin at Hope. "A friendship made in heaven."

Chapter Sixteen

Except the LORD build the house, they labour in vain that build it; except the LORD keep the city, the watchman waketh but in vain.
Psalm 127:1

Hope
The following weekend

Matthew is one of those oblivious men, unaware of their attractiveness. Hope admires her husband's features as he sits before her in the dimly lit restaurant. His thick, dark eyebrows frame his deep hazel eyes, with eyelashes that her female high school classmates would have died for. Below his modest nose and thick, dark mustache, her eyes focus on his mouth while he eats and talks. He is chatty, engaging with her, the hostess, and the waiter. His good mood lifts her spirits.

"I don't know why we don't do this more often." Matthew reaches for his glass. "Mom loves watching the kids for us." His eyebrows dip. "What?"

"What, what?"

He wipes his mouth with his napkin. "Do I have food in my mustache again?"

"No, I'm just admiring the view."

Matthew makes a production of checking behind him and then turning back around, a questioning look on his face.

Hope giggles. "You, silly. You are very handsome tonight."

"Must be the Axe body spray, working its magic." He waggles his eyes dramatically.

"Oh, stop it. You haven't worn that junk since we were dating."

Pointing at her plate with his fork, Matthew says, "Is it not good? You've barely touched your food."

"No, everything's delicious." Hope glances down at her plate, then back at her husband. "But you're better."

"Blah, blah, blah." Matthew wipes his bearded mouth with a napkin. "The Sunday School class you're leading is starting soon, isn't it?"

"One more class with Mr. Hamilton before I start my six-week class."

"That's approaching fast, isn't it? I think I know the answer to this, but are you all set? Ready to share John Wesley with your old folks?"

Hope's chest swells thinking of her classmates. "Give me those sweet people over your teenagers any day." She takes a bite of her baked potato, disappointed that she let it get so cool.

"So, ready or not, here you come." Matthew's eyes twinkle with mirth.

"I'm as ready as I'll ever be, I guess." She dabs her mouth with the linen napkin from her lap. "Thanks for the help with scriptures for the lessons. That is definitely one of your areas of expertise."

"I've got some good resources." He pauses his eating and meets her eyes. "Tell me more about your assignment, from the therapist. What did you say the therapy was called, ESP?"

"That's your favorite sports channel."

"Yuck, yuck."

"The therapy is called CBT. I'm supposed to, one." She points with one finger. "Identify the problem. Two." She adds another finger. "Identify my responses to the problem." Hope pauses as the waiter refills their water glasses. Soft background music is drowned out by the murmurs of conversations around them and the clinking of cutlery. "Thank you." Hope returns to gaze into Matthew's warm eyes. "Apparently, my fear of water is actually the fear of death."

Matthew suspends his fork in mid-air. "I guess that makes sense."

"So, help me. What are some of my responses?"

Matthew takes a bite and answers with a full mouth. "Refusal to be near or on any body of water."

She inhales through her nose as she reaches for her water. She definitely got that one right. There's one response she needn't write down.

After taking a sip, Hope nods. "Sure. What else?"

Matthew takes his time to think as he chews, then points at his plate with the fork. "This is really good. Okay, what else? Um. The yearly nightmares?"

She shakes her head. "I can't control those, so they don't count."

"I know you can't control them, but wouldn't they still be considered responses?"

Hope grabs her fork and takes a stab at a green bean. "I read that the dreams are manifestations of my thought processes and my repressed memories. I can be determined not to remember during the daytime, but when I'm sleeping, I can't control that. Think of my physical reactions. Shaky hands, stuff like that. The things you hear me say."

"Excuse me." Their waiter stands between them. "Would you care for a box for that, ma'am?" He indicates Hope's plate.

"Yes, please." She drops the bean-bearing fork on her plate before allowing it to be whisked away.

"And may I interest you in some dessert, perhaps some coffee?"

Hope lifts her eyes to Matthew, who dramatically waggles his eyebrows. "Maybe both?"

After placing her order for dessert, Hope resumes. "So?"

"Shaky hands, yeah, sometimes. Mostly, though, you pretty much shut down." He lowers his voice, even though they both know no one around them cares to listen. "I've seen you get a distant look in your eyes as if you're far away. Like you've gone someplace I can't follow."

Hope tries to picture how he must have seen her. She must seem pathetic to him.

"As far as things you say, Hope, you pretty much shut down. You have difficulty speaking or expressing how you feel."

"Wow."

"I don't think you can help it."

Another shake of her head. "I can't. But it's good to know how I must appear from the outside. So, what else?"

Matthew finishes his drink and sets it back on the

table, staring at it. "You blame yourself, for the accident, when you shouldn't." When he lifts his eyes to hers, they are no longer dancing. "You were only a kid."

She feels her cheeks heat up, and she swallows. *Nana. I'm so sorry.*

Quiet settles between them as the waiter brings her dessert and a box with her leftovers. While he pours the coffee, she smiles faintly. "Thank you." She doctors the steaming liquid with sugar and cream and takes a sip before she speaks. "Matthew, you're not wrong. I do blame myself. But I guess the blame is ingrained in me. I can't merely tell myself that it's not my fault."

"One of those beliefs that you have to work through."

"Exactly." Hope takes another sip.

"I'm proud of you, you know."

Hope's head shoots up, and her mouth drops open. This is the second time those words have been uttered by him in so many days. She knows he loves her, but she wants to make him proud. Tears well up in her eyes.

Before she can think of a reply, Matthew continues. "Just recognizing you have a problem is a big accomplishment. Seeking professional help is a huge step." His eyes smile, glowing with a warmth that melts her. "I believe in you, and I'll help you however I can."

His image swims before her. Hope has no voice.

"Before you know it, you'll be able to go boating with us. Right?"

Hope's eyes release tears. She covers her face with her napkin. Her hands tremble as she sobs into the fabric, attempting to silence their sounds. She doesn't want others or the waiter to hear, to draw any attention.

"Hon?" Matthew has dropped the volume of his voice. "I'm sorry, I didn't mean to upset you."

Hope shakes her head and takes a deep breath before removing the napkin. She raises her chin, her eyes darting from one side to another before turning back to Matthew. She sees the concern in his eyes and whispers, "I'm sorry."

He shakes his head. "No, honey, don't be sorry. Are you alright? Should we go on home?"

The following week

She isn't as hesitant to see the therapist this time, though Hope still arrives too early and spends time sitting in her car reviewing her journal. Between Matthew, Debbie, and herself, she is confident in what she has written. She was reminded of her schooldays, preparing to hand in homework.

In the office, Hope sits with purpose, her back against the chair this time, a practiced smile on her face after passing her journal to Rachel with a flourish. "I think you will find I have spent the week filling out my answers."

The journal remains closed. "That's good," Rachel says. "How did you feel as you explored your thoughts, beliefs, emotions, and images?"

Hope points to the journal. "I wrote those things down."

Rachel offers a diplomatic smile. "No, how did

you feel as you did the assignment?"

"Oh." Great. *Feelings.* "Well, when I finished, I felt accomplished."

"That's a start. Did you see how your physical responses related to those things?"

"Yes."

"The goal is to change your responses to uncomfortable events. Right now, you probably feel you don't have control over your responses. But being able to acknowledge them is the first step in conquering them. And then, you will change them."

Red splotches appear on Rachel's open neckline. The soft ticking of the clock accompanies Hope as she clasps her hands and refocuses on the journal resting in Rachel's lap, still unopened. "I understand."

Rachel holds the journal towards her. "Very good. So, let's delve further into it."

Her eyebrows draw together. "Aren't you going to read it?"

"What? Oh, the journal? No, this is for you, not for me."

"Oh." Hope takes her journal with reluctance.

"You are disappointed?"

Hope locks eyes with Rachel. "Yes. I guess I'm used to homework being graded."

Rachel laughs. "That's understandable. Thus, assignment, right? No, the journal is yours to use. You can learn to use these techniques for all kinds of issues. Now, let's delve deeper into the cause of your perceived problem."

Hope tilts her head. "Perceived?"

"Tell me about the accident."

Hope clamps her mouth shut. Her heart races.

She's glad that she has a tight grip on the journal with both hands, for fear that her hands would shake otherwise. She drops her gaze.

"Hope?"

"I'm not ready."

"You've spent a week thinking about the thoughts, beliefs, emotions, and images you have relating to the accident, but are hesitant to walk me through what happened?"

Hope nods. Her right leg bounces in rhythm with her racing heartbeat. Hesitant is as good a word as any.

Rachel jots on her legal pad. Hope assumes she is writing something like, *This chick is crazy.*

"How old were you?"

Hope wets her lips. "Thirteen."

"And you were on a body of water?"

"A lake. But, honestly, I don't want to talk about it."

"I understand that, Hope. But *why* don't you want to talk about it?"

"Because I nearly died!" Hope had raised her voice and was leaning forward. "I was thrown from the boat by a big wave, and I didn't have a life jacket on, and if it hadn't been for Nana, I wouldn't *be* here today."

Rachel gives her an expressionless look. Embarrassed by her outburst, Hope lowers her head. Her lips quiver. What is wrong with me? Tears stream from her eyes.

"Here you go." Rachel hands her one of the boxes of tissues.

Her emotions shift to a sense of silliness, and Hope huffs out a short laugh as she remembers noticing the many boxes of tissues during her first visit. "So, that's why you have so many."

"Our faces tend to leak when we get emotional, don't they?" Rachel sets the tissue box back on the coffee table. "Do the dreams produce the same kind of responses as that did?"

Hope's eyes narrow as she thinks. "Yes."

"Do you feel comfortable talking about the dream?"

"Better than the accident itself, yes."

"Tell me about the thoughts, beliefs—"

"Emotions and images."

Rachel nods and offers a small smile. "Yes."

"I relive the accident. In the dream. There's a storm. The water is choppy. A wave hits the boat, and then I'm in the water and falling down, down. When I find I can't hold my breath any longer, warm, strong hands lift me to the surface."

"Good. What are your thoughts then?"

"I'm going to die."

"But do you?"

Hope shakes her head.

"Beliefs?"

"That if I had not been saved, I would be dead."

"But are you?"

"No."

"Emotions?"

Cold. Gripping cold. A sinking sensation. "Fear. Terror."

"Good. What else?"

Hope swallows. "A sense that I am out of control. I am not in command of the situation I find myself in."

"Images?"

"Darkness surrounding me, water pressing down on me. And then, a light, as if from heaven."

"Pressing down is more of a sensation than an image. So, what are the responses you have associated with these things?"

Hope opens her mouth to answer but is interrupted by the jangling of Rachel's cell phone, signaling the end of their session. Rachel's demeanor shifts. The smile fades as she shuts off the alarm. "That's all we have time for this week, I'm afraid. Hope, feel free to write down the responses you have associated with your identified beliefs in your journal, and we'll go over those at your next appointment." Rachel hands her a sheet of paper. "Here's next week's assignment. You must identify a big trigger for you and then challenge yourself."

"Big trigger?" Hope doesn't like the sound of that.

"Something that you would usually avoid that would trigger the beliefs you identified." Rachel opens her calendar. "I'm out of town all next week, so we'll have to schedule for two weeks out. That should give you plenty of time."

"A big trigger." Hope repeats this, feeling quite overwhelmed.

"You don't have to go for a boat ride in a thunderstorm." Rachel tilts her head, an amused look on her face. "But no dipping your toe in the water, either. Jump right into the deep end. Challenge those thoughts, beliefs -"

Hope stands. "All right, I get it. See you in a couple of weeks."

Chapter Seventeen

*And whosoever shall not receive you, nor hear
your words, when ye depart out of that house or city,
shake off the dust of your feet.*
Matthew 10:14

John Wesley
Oxford, England
24 August, 1744

For centuries, St. Mary's Church was the very heart of Oxford University. As the town and university expanded, so did the buildings within.

John Wesley had entered Oxford University at age seventeen, was ordained as a deacon at twenty-two, and at twenty-three was elected as a fellow of Lincoln College. He was twenty-five when he was ordained a priest of the Anglican Church. Oxford was not solely his alma mater. It had long been his security, his comfort, his home.

St. Mary's sanctuary consistently possessed a reverent quiet, yet now the silence was so deep that John could swear he was deaf were it not for the echoes of his footfalls. It was as if the building itself held its breath. He paused briefly, gazing at the backs of the heads of those seated in the pews, before stepping forward down the center aisle. John approached the lectern with his eyes downcast, as a condemned man might make his way to the gallows.

If Father could only see me now.

Samuel Wesley would be gravely disappointed, sternly advising his son against delivering the sermon that John clutched in his left hand. Less of a sermon, though. The words were more of a treatise. At least he wasn't going to nail it to the door of St. Mary's as if he were a modern-day Martin Luther.

John Wesley was about to commit academic suicide.

He laid the papers on the lectern and stared down at the swimming words. John was certain this would be his final sermon here. He assumed it would be the last time he stepped foot in this beloved sanctuary.

Since his conversion six years prior, his eyes were opened to the issues in the church. It must be natural for institutions to devolve into a set of rule-creators and followers. Strict methods established boundaries, and John had always been a good rule-follower. However, once the Spirit directed him to think beyond the boundaries and urged him to preach, not only outside his assigned area but even outside church buildings, John possessed a different perspective. He had begun to question, as had Martin Luther before him, the scriptural basis of some of the church's doctrine.

His mantra had become, 'But is it scriptural?'

John Wesley lifted his head from the pages before him to observe those filling the pews. The black and white of their garb mimicked the checkerboard tiles of the flooring. There sat his superiors, his instructors, their arms crossed and their eyebrows drawn. Their eyes cold as ice.

Wesley tore his attention from them and returned to the careful handwriting of his message, enumerating each of the points he intended to make. He opened his mouth and read the first scripture from the book of the prophet Ezekiel.

"Whosoever heareth the sound of the trumpet and taketh not warning; if the sword come and take him away, his blood shall be upon his own head."

John had a sudden vision, that of Saint Paul at the Temple for the last time, being dragged out by angry men, set on putting him to death. While the group before him was above violence, John's removal would be, nonetheless, every bit as permanent.

Before beginning his sermon, John read from the book of Acts. "And they were all filled with the Holy Ghost."

John continued reading, occasionally lifting his head from the pages. The black robes remained like statues—no expression, their stony eyes boring into him.

He built his argument by examining the establishment of the Christian faith, extensively using scripture to support his statements, particularly the words of Saint Paul. In the early days, the believers were of one heart and one soul. He explained how Christianity spread, person by person, throughout the known world. However, men of pleasure, those of the world, were offended, and persecution of the believers abounded.

"But the Father has ordained that the entire world shall become a Christian world," John argued. "Imagine that the fullness of time has arrived and the prophecies accomplished, what a wonderful world! Wars have ceased, there is no civil discord, no oppression, no thievery, no injustice."

John took a deep breath. As his right hand reached to turn the page, a familiar warmth enveloped him, like a strong arm draped around his shoulder. A sense of peace filled him, a belief that, no matter what happened, he was loved and had followed Christ's command.

"Having thus briefly considered Christianity," John continued, "it remains only that I should close the whole with a plain, practical application.

"First, I would ask, where does such Christianity now exist?"

Wesley read. He used eleven points to persuade his listeners. In point five, he repeated the question posed to him years earlier. "Are you filled with the Holy Ghost? Are your thoughts, your desires, your words, your actions consistent with what God has displayed to you?" Point six convicted them as teachers, instructors of future shepherds of their flocks. What did they teach through their example?

The more John convicted them, the more they squirmed, as if statues had come to life, exchanging glances with their neighbors, barely concealing their displeasure with him.

By point ten, John charged forward as if the very fire of God burned within him. "So many of you are a generation of triflers, triflers with God, with one another, and with your own souls. How few of you spend a single hour in private prayer? Who of you is acquainted with the work of the Spirit? Do you allow talk of the Holy Ghost in a church, or do you condemn it as 'enthusiasm'?"

The faces of his audience blazed red. Many heads shook, and they whispered among themselves. John pictured how the Pharisees must have behaved as Jesus rebuked them.

Wesley concluded with a plea to God to save them and help them, as He alone is able. "Only God can restore the church, and the leadership and direction of not only Oxford but of the entire Church of England, which can only be restored to a scriptural faith by God alone."

John's raised voice echoed with his final word. He dipped his chin. Once the last remnant of his voice was swallowed by the sanctuary's high ceiling, all that remained was the sound of his ragged breath. He gathered his pages, and John Wesley turned away, stepping from the lectern for the last time.

Chapter Eighteen

*Jesus, lover of my soul, let me to thy bosom fly,
while the nearer waters roll, while the tempest still is
high; hide me, O my Savior, hide, till the storm of life is
past; safe into the haven guide, O receive my soul at
last!*
Charles Wesley

Hope
The weekend following her second therapy session

The hotel is not crowded, but perhaps that's because they arrived on a Thursday night. Matthew took Friday off work, and Hope notified the school that Eric and Sam would be absent the following day for a mini family vacation. They don't have much schooling left at this point in May anyway, she reasoned. After the therapy session, Matthew helped her brainstorm and create a two-night schedule of activities designed to provide varying degrees of potential stimuli for her anxiety. Rachel had warned her against choosing easier activities or trying to gradually increase the intensity of the triggers. "Studies show that CBT exposures of varying intensity are far more effective," she'd reported.

So it was that Hope and Matthew decided that a hotel pool and watching deep-water themed movies could cross off a few such items. They had agreed not to refer to the list as 'triggers,' so as not to overly concern the children. Surrounded by her family, Hope believes she can manage to get through it.

After hauling their suitcases and overnight bags to their hotel room, the four of them headed out for an early supper. A nearby Cracker Barrel restaurant proved to be the perfect spot for a cozy meal and lively discussion.

After the waitress takes their orders, Matthew pulls a folded paper from his shirt pocket. "So, kids. Your mom has indicated that one thing that bothers her a lot is watching any films with storms."

Eric's dark eyes widen. "Like 'Twister'?"

"No." Matthew draws out the word. "Storms at sea."

"Oh." Eric's face falls. "I want to see the cow flying through the air."

Hope grins at her son. "Yeah, that's a good one. Unrealistic, but still fun."

Matthew unfolds the paper and places it on the table like a placemat. "There are four movies to choose from. We may not get through all of them in the next day or two, but we're going to try."

Samantha turns concerned eyes toward her mother, her brows drawn. "Are you gonna be okay, Mom? I mean, will they make you cry?"

Sweet Sam, worried for me. "No, honey. If you don't cry, I won't cry."

Eric wrinkles his nose. "Why would you cry?

There's not any mushy stuff, is there?"

Hope wrinkles her nose. "Gosh, I don't know. I've never seen them."

Matthew furrows his brows. "I don't remember. I don't think so." He gestures toward the list. "They're all rated either PG or PG-13. And I don't think they're romantic. Well." He clears his throat. "Any more romantic than 'Twister,' anyway. The point is that each involves deep water or storms at sea. Your mom wants you two to pick the one we'll watch tonight when we return to the hotel, and then the next one for the morning."

Samantha sticks out her bottom lip. "I thought we were gonna swim in the pool. That's why we're going to the hotel in the first place."

Hope places a hand on her daughter's crossed arms and nods. "That's on the agenda, too, dear."

"But, Mom," Eric interrupts. "You don't swim."

Matthew winks at his son. "She is this weekend, Eric." He taps the paper with his index finger. "At least, that's the plan."

Hope removes her hand from her daughter and leans conspiratorially across the table toward Eric, wide-eyed. She whispers harshly, "I even bought a brand-new swimsuit, solely for this time together."

Eric's mouth falls into an 'o.'

"Anyway," Matthew says, "we'll show you two the trailers to all four of the movies, and you guys will pick out the one to watch tonight. How does that sound?"

The waitress brings their food, and Matthew refolds the list and slips it back into his pocket. His eyes meet his wife's, and she notices the bright hope shining in them, with a satisfied grin spreading across his face. She feeds off his oozing confidence.

They were going to have a wonderful weekend. She can sense it.

At supper, Matthew asks her about the Sunday School class, her portion of which had started the previous weekend. Although he had briefly inquired about it on Sunday, she sensed he wanted to help build her self-confidence. The first class covered background information about the Wesley family and John's rescue from the burning house.

"The next class is about Wesley's schooling and the Holy Club at Oxford."

"The storm in the Atlantic then—"

"I'm saving that for week three."

"Halfway through the class."

Hope nods. "Yep. I'm likely to be 'livin' on a prayer' myself by then."

Matthew laughs. "Different John, my love."

The Gerards successfully exit the restaurant without purchasing any candy or toys for their children and head back to the hotel. When the elevator dings and the doors slide open to their floor, Eric dashes out.

"Race ya!" he shouts as the two of them run, stomping down the hallway.

"I don't know why they do that." Matthew extracts the room key from his wallet. "They know they'll have to wait for us."

Once in the room, Matthew signs in to their online movie account and finds the trailers. Hope is relieved when the kids choose 'The Abyss,' despite a short scene in the trailer that features a kiss. She, of course, has never seen it, but at least it doesn't show a storm at sea. She assumes that makes it the least worrisome.

They all change into their pajamas and tumble onto the beds. With Matthew's hand in hers, she questions why he suggested the film as a potential trigger. But as the story progresses, she understands. In the first drowning scene, when the main characters are in the flooding vessel, the water rises, and they argue about how to proceed. When the female character suggests that she has to drown in the chilling waters, Hope's heart races. She closes her eyes and feels the weight of the water around her body. Matthew clasps her hand and leans over to speak softly in her ear. "It's a movie, honey. It's just a movie. Breathe. Remember? In through your nose, out through your mouth."

"The kids." Her voice barely vocalizes.

"They're engrossed. Don't worry."

She squeezes her eyelids tight but can still hear what is happening in the film, despite the roaring in her ears. Her hands sweat as she focuses on her breathing, her husband's murmurs a deep drone in her ear, anchoring her through the scene. Her lips move as she inwardly recites the Lord's Prayer with Matthew. The chill within her gradually gives way to a reassuring warmth. When the scene ends, her heart rate slows, and she cautiously cracks open her eyelids. Instead of checking the visions on the television screen, she turns to Matthew. His deep, dark eyes are filled with warmth.

"There," he says, patting her hand, "that wasn't so bad, was it?"

She tilts her head and takes a deep ragged breath. "That was killer."

Matthew throws his arm around her, and they watch the remainder of the film.

The children lie on their stomachs at the foot of the hotel bed, resting their chins on their open palms while movie number two plays on the television screen. Matthew sits at Hope's side on the bed, propped up with several pillows behind their backs, his hand once again engulfing hers.

"You did great last evening." Matthew's fingers squeeze as he half-whispers to her.

Hope grimaces. "Does clamping your eyes shut count as 'watching' a movie?" She relishes the warmth of him, so near and reassuring. "But thanks. I did a lot better than I would have if I were here alone." She huffs at the thought. "Well, honestly, I would have turned it over to a comedy, all on dry land. Actually, I'd probably fare better with a horror film in a spooky old house."

"You did rank watching movies as a higher risk trigger than swimming in a hotel pool." Matthew takes in their children at the end of the bed, engrossed in the old 1970s *Poseidon Adventure*. "I'm surprised they tolerate these shows."

Eric had declared the film "cheesy," as if he were a twelve-year-old film critic. But from the moment the giant cruise ship capsizes, he becomes enthralled. Samantha is more antsy than her older brother, eager to go swimming, her swimsuit already on and her legs kicking the bedspread. Hope does better with this movie more, probably because of its age. Shirley Winters cracking jokes after diving in to save someone else feels a little too close to home, though she doubts very much that Nana had time to do the same.

"Mom?" Samantha jumps up from the bed as soon as the end credits roll. "Get your suit on. Come on, I wanna go!"

Hope laughs as she swings her legs to sit on the edge of the bed. "Okay, okay! Shut it off, Eric, and get your trunks on. Dad, you too."

Minutes later, the four of them step out of the elevator. Hope had forgotten how annoying flip-flops sound on a tiled floor. As they approach the pool area, the muffled shouts of children drift toward her. This is gonna be a breeze.

As the steamy door to the pool swings open, the commotion of boisterous, splashing children hits her like a wave. The entire pool area is surrounded by glass on three sides, save for the ceiling and the adjacent hotel wall. Eric and Samantha dash to a table, kick off their flip-flops, and scamper toward the pool.

"Walk, don't run!" Matthew has to raise his voice over the din. Half a dozen other children bob in the pool. Hope surveys the area around her and spots a lone adult sitting on a lounger, her nose in a book, dressed in street clothes.

Hope murmurs to her husband, "This is so annoying. Those kids are essentially unaccompanied."

Matthew smiles down at her. "No worries, honey. They aren't our responsibility."

The Gerard children both jump into the pool, creating the biggest splash they can manage.

"You've already gotten farther than you have in the past, sweetheart."

"True." As a rule, Hope stayed in the hotel room and read. Or better yet, she went shopping, leaving

Matthew with one hundred percent of the swim-time supervision. The thought of entering the pool area usually gave her heart palpitations. But now she was not only in the pool area but also sported a one-piece swimsuit, the first one she had purchased as an adult. And she was here with the full intention of getting in the pool, too.

Before the accident, she loved being in and around water. As a child, Hope and her grandparents often stayed at their lake house. They would go boating and skiing, frequently anchoring the boat in a cove to swim. She didn't even mind when fish nibbled at her toes. Being in the water felt second nature to her back then. Papa often declared she was part fish, as she was drawn to water wherever she found it. Even a puddle in the street attracted her like a magnet.

That is, until the accident. Since then, the only water that has touched her body was in a shower.

The shouts of delight from her children made her smile. Compared to watching movies, which always felt so real to her, this was easy. A heated hotel swimming pool, three to four and a half feet deep, with its stench of chlorine and little kids, is as remote from a lake during a thunderstorm as she could possibly get.

A walk in the park.

The bright mid-morning May sky that had greeted her as they stepped into the pool area turns overcast, like a giant shadow skittering across the great expanse. Hope frowns. "I didn't know it was forecast to rain."

Matthew glances at them. "I don't think it was, but it sure looks like it." Then he offers her a mischievous grin. "Good thing this is an indoor pool, huh?" He points to her feet. "Best kick off those lovely new flip-flops and get your new swimsuit wet."

Her husband grips her arm as they step toward the pool. The fluorescent lighting takes over as the glassed-in area darkens around them. Her heart starts revving up, but Hope takes note of it. A racing heart is one of the usual responses to a trigger. This response can be changed. Rumbling interrupts her mantra, accentuated by rain pounding on the roof.

"Wow, that came on fast!" Hope approaches the pool's shallow end, while Matthew uses both hands to guide and support her. Her hands are sticky from sweat. Check. This is just another one of your old responses.

"Don't think about what's going on outside, sweetheart. We're not out there. Concentrate on me and where your feet are. You've got this." Matthew's hands are warm with their firm, steady grip.

Hope places her lead foot on the first step, and the warm water swirls around as she lowers her other foot to stand ankle-deep in the pool.

Her daughter swims nearby, a wide smile on her face. "Mom! You're in the pool!" Samantha stands and turns to shout at her brother. "Eric, look at Momma."

Eric stands next to the pool at the far end, his mouth open. "Mom!" Hope strains to hear him over the echoes of shouting children, the splashing water, the rain pouring heavily on the roof above her, and the rumbles of thunder. But she can read her title form in his mouth. Warmth rises within her, chasing away the writhing cold.

Hope takes two more steps into the water. As more of her body is submerged, her goosebumps become more pronounced. Despite the rainstorm outside pounding against the glass panes behind him,

Hope maintains her focus on her son at the deep end of the pool, not allowing her attention to drift to the rising water around her. She observes her breathing. In through the nose, out through the mouth. Her heart rate gradually slows.

I can do this. I am *doing this.*

Two things happen simultaneously. A giant crack of lightning flashes outside the window, instantly followed by a loud boom of thunder. At the exact same moment, a huge splash of pool water pours over Hope. She screams in terror. Matthew's arms surround her immediately, holding her close as she wails into his chest. There is a roaring in her ears, and all the once-deafening sounds become distant and muffled. Hope shakes and cries while the world spins around her as her legs give way.

She doesn't remember getting out of the pool or how she managed to lie on one of the loungers, wrapped in towels, with her husband kneeling on the floor, stroking her forehead with one hand and holding her right hand with the other.

She meets her husband's eyes, which are filled with worry. "Oh, Matthew." Hope sobs. "I'm so sorry."

"You're okay, baby. Everything's fine." He bends over her so she can see his entire face. "We will get through this. I promise."

Chapter Nineteen

*No marvel then, that the great mystery of the
gospel should be now also hid from the wise and
prudent, as well as in the days of old; that it should be
almost universally denied, ridiculed and exploded as
mere frenzy: and that all who dare avow it still, are
branded with the names of madmen and enthusiasts.*
John Wesley

Hope
The following week

"I really must invest in an umbrella." Hope says
this after pulling back the dripping hood of her jacket.

"There's a coat rack behind you." Hope's
therapist points to the wall. "Feel free to hang your
jacket there."

The room where they always meet is just as
cheerful as during her previous visits, featuring fresh
flowers in a vase and the pleasant aroma wafting from a
diffuser. The floor lamp in the corner provides the only
light, while the outdoor gloom darkens the windows.

"Have a seat, Hope." Rachel places a fresh box of

tissues on the coffee table between them before setting the familiar legal pad on her lap. She removes a pencil from behind her ear. "How did it go this last weekend? I know you had a big one planned, with several different levels of exposure."

Hope stares at Rachel's legal pad. "It started out great. We saw a couple of movies together. That went fine. I think the pool would have been okay, too, but there was a storm. It came on strong the moment I got in the pool." Hope sighs and raises her eyes to Rachel, who tilts her head.

"A storm?"

"Yes. A big one. A thunderstorm. Lightning, thunder, dark skies."

"It's raining outside now, Hope. Does the rain bother you?"

Hope shakes her head. "No, it's not that it was raining or that it was dark outside. Rain was blowing hard against the windows of the pool area, and a loud crack of lightning struck something nearby, and I was splashed in the face with water. All at the same time. And I—well, I freaked out."

Rachel scribbles on her legal pad. Hope grits her teeth at the sound of the pencil scratching.

"That's good, Hope." Her therapist gives her an encouraging look. "That was a huge exposure, and you lived through it, didn't you?"

Hope opens her mouth but then closes it. Rain patters against the window, and the clock ticks louder than she remembers from previous visits.

"Hope?"

Hope makes eye contact with her therapist. "I was hoping you might understand how that experience made me feel." Irritation had settled over her like an itch without a rash. "It was horrible, Rachel. Thank God Matthew was right there with me, to help me through the panic."

Rachel places the pencil down on the legal pad. "You didn't answer my question, Hope. You didn't die, did you? We live through panic attacks. The more you experience, the more you will realize that your body, your brain, is reacting in a learned way. You need to teach it to react, or rather, to respond in a different way. You see, your autonomic nervous system is telling you there is imminent danger. But there was no threat. You said yourself that Matthew was there. So, a part of you acknowledges that you were not in any real jeopardy. Do you understand?

Hope takes another deep breath and folds her hands in her lap. She shifts her focus from Rachel's face to the therapist's hands, noting the chewed nails and the angry flesh at the fingertips. "I've been reading a lot about CBT, as you suggested. I've also run across something called EMDR, which is the eye movement thing. Do you think that might be helpful for me?"

Rachel's brows furrow, and her voice has developed a sharp edge. "Who's the therapist here, Hope? You've met with me for my expert advice. I believe CBT is the best therapy right now for your death anxiety." She retrieves the pencil. "It is not until you fully understand your problems with death that you will conquer your fear of it. Death will then have no control over you or your body."

"Are you sure that's what this is for me, death anxiety?"

"Yes, Hope. I have treated many people and have

conducted considerable research and training in this field. Death anxiety plagues our society; in fact, it has affected humankind for as long as humans have existed. Some fear the unknown, others fear leaving no legacy, and yet some fear the nothingness of death. They struggle to accept that this life is all there is and that death is simply a part of that existence."

Blinking, Hope lets her mouth fall open. It's her turn to tilt her head. "Nothingness? Are you saying what I think you're saying?"

Rachel sits upright. "There is absolutely no scientific evidence of an afterlife. This life is all there is."

Hope cannot help but let out a small laugh. "You're being serious."

Rachel's mouth sets in a straight line. No response.

"What is wind, Rachel?" Hope asks. "Can you see it, or merely the effects of it? Can you see the warmth that emanates from a loved one as they see you approach, or do you only feel it? We are energy, Rachel, and these bodies merely house our souls, our energy, here in the physical world. Death is not the end of our existence. It is the gateway to another existence, to what lies beyond. What's more—"

"There is no evidence."

"That you have researched. That you have been taught. Do you know what would happen to your industry if the lie of 'nothingness' were not propagated? I'm pretty sure I do." Rachel's head bows. "God doesn't need my defense. There's what I know, and then there's this thing called 'faith.' I believe in heaven. I believe in God." Hope stands. "And I believe, Rachel, that our session is over for today."

Rachel bolts upright, dropping her chewed pencil on the floor. "I'm sorry if I insulted your beliefs, Hope. I didn't mean to."

Hope waves a dismissive hand before reaching into her purse for her checkbook, tearing out the prepared check and handing it to Rachel. "For today's session."

As Hope turns toward the door, Rachel calls out to her retreating back. "Wait, you've not made an appointment for next week yet."

Her hand on the doorknob, Hope turns. "I'll think about it and let you know."

As the kids scrape their plates and place them in the dishwasher, Matthew remains seated at the table, his empty plate in front of him. He makes eye contact with her.

"Is everything okay?" he asks. "You've been quiet since I got home."

Hope offers him a small smile. "I had my therapy session today. I'd like to talk to you about it, but—" She glances over at their children as they finish their chores.

Matthew follows her gaze. "Kids, why don't you guys go find something on TV you both like? Mom and I are going to have a grown-up talk."

Eric makes a face. "Well, that sounds boring." He gets a mischievous look on his face. "First one to the remote picks the show!"

"Eric, no!" Samantha chases after him, out of the kitchen.

"Do you want more tea?" Hope rises from the table and reaches to take Matthew's plate from him.

"Would love some, thanks."

After pouring them both more iced tea, Hope sits back down. She watches silently as her husband stirs in sugar and takes a sip.

"So," he says. "The therapist appointment."

"Yeah." She runs a finger along the rim of her glass. "I reported to Rachel about the weekend and how I freaked out."

"You know Eric feels awful about that. He feels it's his fault you panicked."

Hope shakes her head. "I know, I've tried to reassure him. How could he have timed his cannonball precisely when the lightning struck outside the hotel?"

"The perfect storm."

"Exactly. Anyway, when I told her about it, she was, well, literally like that meme from that popular movie. You know the one." She tries to mimic the actor in the film. "But did you die?"

Matthew leans his shoulders toward her, his mouth hanging open. "You're kidding me. She didn't!"

"Oh, yes, she did. She said that's why it's good to challenge the mind with these triggers. Once I can convince myself that I'm not going to die, my brain will start to chill out. Teach the brain something new, that sort of thing."

"I'm not sure I buy that theory."

"I suppose the concept is much like the idea of allergy shots—injecting the very stuff one is allergic to in order to get the body to adjust to it."

"Yeah, but they start small with those and slowly increase the dose." He nods, as if the therapist is in the adjacent room. "That woman doesn't want you to start small." Matthew's eyes bore into hers. "It hurt me to see you so scared, Hope. I don't like the idea of what it must have been like for you."

Hope drops her gaze to the table. She notices a couple of bread crumbs she missed and pushes them aside with her finger. "She said it is important for people to get over their fear of death and acknowledge that there is nothing after life is over."

"What?"

Hope nods as she returns her regard to him. "She said that. She said that the fear of death is silly, as it is merely a part of life. That there is no 'great unknown' because it is known to be, well, nothing." Her husband's brows knit together, his handsome mouth set in a straight line. "I know. I even laughed a little at her. I thought she couldn't be serious. But she was. She was dead serious."

Matthew leans back in his chair, his mouth open but speechless.

"I told her I believe very much in an afterlife, that our souls are eternal, and that there is most definitely something after death. And then, I stood and ended the session. Gave her the check and walked out without making another appointment. Basically, I told her, don't call me, I'll call you."

The kitchen is quiet. The audio from the television in the living room seeps in from the side. Hope notices her husband's expression and frowns.

She drops her voice low. "Are you mad at me?"

Matthew shakes his head and blinks. "No. No, I'm not." He offers his own small smile. "You stood up for yourself and your faith. Are you kidding? Mad? No,

I'm proud of you. You did the absolute right thing. I'm just a bit shocked."

"Rachel gave me a shallow apology, said she didn't mean to challenge my beliefs or something like that. Matthew." She straightens her back. "I'm not sure this is the right kind of therapy for me. Maybe I should seek a different counselor."

With his elbows on the table, Matthew forms a tent with his hands and leans them against his lips. After a brief pause, he speaks.

"Maybe this is more of a faith matter than a mental thing. Maybe you don't need a therapist at all. I mean, we can continue to do the CBT. But let's face it. If it's more a matter of faith, perhaps we should meet with Pastor Robert and see what he thinks of it all."

Hope considers this for a moment but then gives her head a curt shake. "No, I don't want to do that to him. I know he'd be happy to listen, but I really don't feel like having to tell the whole dreadful story of the accident with him." Matthew's mouth opens, she assumes, to argue. She lifts her hand, bending her wrist on the table. "I should feel comfortable with him knowing, of course. I understand that. He is our pastor after all. But I simply don't feel like dredging it all up and risking a panic attack telling him about it. I would feel awful."

Matthew's eyes twinkle. "I know who we should speak to."

"What? Who?"

"Don't you still send a Christmas card to your childhood pastor?"

Hope's mouth opens. "Pastor Dave?"

"That's the one. The guy who married us."

"Do you think he would meet with me?"

"Of course, he will. He loves you."

Memories flood Hope then: those of children's sermons, communion, and confirmation class. Pastor Dave had been a rock for their family, both before and especially after the accident. He retired shortly before Hope and Matthew's wedding but agreed to perform the ceremony for her. For them. She wouldn't have to tell him about the accident. He already knew.

Her face breaks into a broad grin. "Matthew, you're a genius. You know that?"

"You're lucky to have me."

She laughs. "Indeed, I am. I'll call him tomorrow and see if he will meet us."

Chapter Twenty

But the Master of the Sea heard my despairing
cry,
From the waters lifted me, now safe am I.
James Rowe

Hope
The following Friday evening

Jake and Barnie's restaurant buzzes with patrons, their laughter and conversations punctuated by the clinking of silverware on plates. The tinkling of the grand piano serves less as background music and more like a filler for the breathing space. Hope and Matthew sit at their paper-lined table, linen napkins resting on their laps. Matthew holds his glass of tea, swirls it, and takes a whiff.

"Mmm, this has a great nose. I'm guessing this is a recently made pitcher of tea."

Hope grins at her poor imitation of a wine connoisseur. She surveys the room and notices only one open table. "Good thing we made reservations. I don't know how long we'd have to wait to be seated without them."

"I'm glad we intentionally told Pastor Dave

fifteen minutes later than the reservation. That man is chronically early." Matthew wags his head.

"You say that as if it were a bad thing."

"I didn't want him waiting on us. This feels better to me."

Hope spots her childhood pastor weaving between tables, obediently following the hostess toward them. "Speaking of, here he is."

They both rise from their seats to greet their guest. Hope notices a slight shuffle of the man's feet and a bit of a bow at his shoulders. Yet, his eyes are warm, framed by white eyebrows. Matthew extends his hand, but Hope opens her arms to embrace the elderly man.

"I've heard about this place." The man who married Hope and Matthew smiles as he takes a seat. "I'm glad to have the chance to try it."

"We like it a lot, Pastor." Matthew takes a sip of water before continuing. "I'm glad you don't have to drive very far. It's kind of strange that you ended up retiring and moving this close to us."

"Coincidence?" Pastor Dave winks at Hope. "I think not." He smiles at Matthew. "No, this area had been a favorite for family vacations for years. It seemed natural to make it a permanent home."

Hope observes the slight tremor of his right hand, the thumb rubbing rhythmically against the pads of its neighbors before Pastor Dave picks up the faux leather-covered menu lying before him. "This is a menu? I feel like I'm in a classroom. Will there be a quiz before we can order?"

One thing that had not aged in the man was his voice. He possessed a deep voice that resonated over the noise of the bustling restaurant.

"Thanks for meeting with us." Hope fiddles with the silverware lying in wait. "Matthew and I really value your opinion."

"As well as enjoy your company," Matthew adds.

After the waitress takes their order, Pastor Dave holds his coffee mug with both hands. "Is there something you are not comfortable discussing with your current pastor?"

Hope studies Pastor Dave's hands. Holding the cup, there is no sign of a tremor. The veins are prominent, and the bronzed skin is thin. Though he has been widowed for several years, he wears his gold wedding band on his left hand. "It's not that we don't trust him, of course we do. But, well, you're the one who has known me for so long. You counseled us before we married. You officiated our wedding."

Matthew grasps Hope's hand and settles it on the table. "Don't misunderstand. Pastor Robert is great. He simply doesn't know Hope like you do."

Hope lowers her voice. "Or know about my past."

Pastor Dave nods. "I see. So, what is it you want to discuss?"

Hope senses her husband's scrutiny, yet she feels the gaze of Pastor Dave and recognizes the warmth in those gray eyes. The background music of the restaurant envelops her like a blanket, with soft murmurs of conversation, silverware clinking against ceramic, and sounds wafting from the kitchen. "I'm not sure where to begin."

Matthew squeezes her hand. "Maybe start with the dreams."

"Yes, of course." Hope takes a sip of her water, wetting her lips that have become dry. "I've had the same dream now for years, usually around the time of the anniversary of the accident."

Pastor Dave gives a small nod. "Ah, yes. The boating accident, when you were young."

"Yes, when I was thirteen."

"I remember it well." Her former pastor waves his hand. "Please, go on."

"The dream is not always the same, but each one is very similar. I am in the water, immersed and confused, and struggling to find the surface. When I think I can't hold my breath any longer, I am raised upward, from below."

"She wakes up gasping for breath as if it were real."

"This happens every year?"

"For as long as I can remember."

"How old were you when they started?"

Hope breaks his gaze. How long *has* it been? "I don't remember exactly."

The conversation pauses as they are served salads and offered black pepper. Matthew doesn't stop the waitress until the top of his Caesar salad is black. Hope raises her eyebrows at him, but he offers her a lopsided grin and shrugs his shoulders. Pastor Dave pretends not to notice as he spreads his napkin on his lap and then lifts his head.

"Matthew, Hope. Let's pray over the food and our time together, shall we?" Pastor Dave closes his eyes and clasps his hands together. "Lord, we thank you for this food, for this beautiful evening, and for our time together. Bless Matthew and Hope and their children, and grant us all safe travels home. In Jesus's name I pray."

Hope and Matthew join in with their "amen" before reaching for their salad forks. Hope pushes the curls of sliced onion to the edge of her salad plate, partly delaying the conversation about their meeting and partly eager to dive in. She stabs a cherry tomato, and her stomach flips.

"So, Hope." Pastor Dave lowers his voice. "You were saying that you've been having dreams related to the accident." His expression remains neutral, but his kind eyes connect with hers.

The hairs on Hope's arms stand on end, and a shiver begins in her shoulders. She lays her fork on the salad plate and takes a sip of water before she manages to answer. "I wake up in a panic. They're nightmares, really, rather than just dreams. They're terrible."

"She's seen a therapist who diagnosed her with PTSD." Matthew indicates with his fork. "Post Traumatic Stress Disorder. She has even had some attacks merely thinking about storms at sea and shipwrecks."

Hope lowers both hands in her lap and bows her head. Her stomach has soured, and she regrets ordering any food at all.

"That's good, Hope," her former pastor replies. "I'm glad you're getting some therapy. You survived a traumatic experience."

She raises her eyes to his and sees no judgment there.

"May I take that, sir?" The waitress stands next to Matthew, whose cleaned salad plate bears not even a fleck of lettuce.

"Yes, please."

Hope is shocked to note that both men have

finished their salads, while she has done little more than rearrange the greens on her plate.

"Ma'am?" The waitress holds an open palm toward her full plate.

"No, I'll." Hope swallows. "I'll work on it."

"Yes, ma'am. Your orders are coming right out."

Maybe a restaurant wasn't the best place to have this talk. Hope sighs, reaches for her napkin, and dabs at her mouth, even though she hasn't eaten a bite. "Pastor, I have learned a lot from my counselor, and I appreciate the therapy. But Matthew and I, we feel there is something missing. I need to talk about what happened with someone who knew me back then, with me, and Nana, and Papa." She clasps her hands together, still lying on her lap.

"Hope." Matthew gestures with his chin. "The waitress is coming with our entrees."

She nods and waits for the waitress to disappear again. Pastor Dave doesn't lift his fork, while Matthew eagerly digs in, cutting his steak with gusto.

"I've tried to forget about the entire event and its aftermath." Hope speaks into her shrimp skewers atop a bed of rice pilaf. "But the dreams bring back the awfulness every year."

"She blames herself, you know, Pastor." Matthew's voice is soft and tender. "She blames herself for her grandmother's death."

Her former pastor swings his head from Matthew to Hope. "Is this true?"

Hope's lips quiver. "I know I didn't cause the storm, and I had no way of knowing that the wind and waves would throw me overboard." She takes a deep breath. "Nana harped at me to leave my life jacket on. It was uncomfortable and ugly, and I wanted to lie up front on the boat without it." She feels her eyes fill with tears, and her voice breaks as she continues. "If I'd had that stupid thing on, she wouldn't have had to jump in after me."

"Oh, Hope." Pastor Dave says, his words full of empathy.

"Papa was devastated." Tears squeeze out of the corners of Hope's eyes. "He was never the same after that. He tried, I know he did. But we were both lost without her."

A handful of moments passed as the men at the table allowed her time to compose herself. She felt small, as if she had regressed to age thirteen, she and her grandfather navigating the darkness of grief, trying to live in their individual spheres, intersecting only when necessary. She lifted her head to see Matthew's plate empty and Pastor Dave's nearly so.

"My therapist doesn't believe in an afterlife, and that's my biggest issue with the treatment." Hope shakes her head. "Her death anxiety theory seems built on the belief that after death, there is nothing. At this point, I don't feel comfortable with the therapy if my beliefs cannot be integrated with them."

"If I may say so," Matthew interjects, "I wonder if there's some kind of therapy that can incorporate Hope's beliefs. I can see the value in what the therapist is doing, but I'm also concerned about the flooding aspect. If she could gradually increase her triggers and perhaps gain confidence with each victory, no matter how small, maybe that would help her more. It'd be a shame to quit if it has the potential to make a difference." He draws his lips into his mouth and gestures toward his wife. "I hate to see her suffer like this."

Hope gulps. "Pastor, what are your thoughts?"

Their guest doesn't respond until the waitress inquires about take-out containers, asks about dessert, and clears away their dinner plates. Left unattended once more, Pastor Dave spreads his hands wide.

"First of all, Hope, you must understand that your only guilt is of being thirteen years old at the time. Wearing a life jacket would have helped you, but it wouldn't have prevented your grandmother from jumping in after you. Do you understand this?"

Hope gazes at him with tear-filled eyes, her lips trembling. "I suppose so."

"It was instinct that caused Audrey to jump into the turbulent lake after her granddaughter was thrown in by a freak storm." Pastor Dave wipes his mouth with his napkin.

Hope whispers. "She saved me."

Tilting his head, the pastor's brows draw together. "What do you mean, child?"

"Nana got under me and pushed me to the surface. I felt it. I feel it in my dreams, too, like I'm reliving it."

Pastor Dave shakes his head. "Hope, your grandmother jumped in next to the boat and was trapped under it. You were thrown out, away from the boat."

Hope's mouth drops open as she first turns to her husband before returning her attention to the pastor. "What are you saying?"

"I'm saying that after your grandmother jumped in the lake, she must have become disoriented. She was trapped under the boat. There was no way she could have reached you."

"That can't be. Warm hands raised me to the surface of the water."

The hairs on Hope's arms stand on end as a shiver runs down her spine. Her mouth forms a little 'o' as she exchanges a wide-eyed look with her husband. "Are you saying," she questions, slowly, the words sticking on her tongue.

In a hoarse whisper, Matthew expresses what they are all thinking. "Could it have been an angel?"

Pastor Dave lays a trembling, open hand on the table. "Only you know what you felt, Hope."

Hope can feel the warm hands even now, as she conjures the memory, no longer afraid to think of it.

Matthew reaches for her hand. "Sweetheart, does this change things for you?"

"Perhaps. Yeah, maybe. I don't know." Hope addresses her former pastor. "The therapist said my fear of the water is the fear of death. Am I afraid to die?"

Pastor Dave reaches for his coffee. "Good thing this is decaf. Otherwise, I'd be awake all night." He takes a long gulp before resuming. "The fear of death has been the topic of philosophy as long as there have been philosophers. Probably longer. I believe it is referred to as the human condition. But to those of us who believe, we have hope. Something that non-believers, such as your therapist, do not have."

"I believe in heaven, Pastor. You know I do."

"There is a difference between believing and knowing. Do you know Jesus, Hope? Do you walk with Him? Do you know that He died for *you*, for *your* salvation?"

Lord, I believe. Help my unbelief! That line leaps

into Hope's mind.

"Jesus conquered death. He has promised us a place with Him." Pastor Dave reaches toward her, palms up. As she lays her own in his, he continues. "You will have no fear of death when you have peace with God and have a clear vision of the glories awaiting you. Remember the words of the Apostle Paul: Because we are justified by faith, we are at peace with God."

Hope smiles at one of her favorite passages. "Jesus does give us hope, doesn't He?"

"Live in His word, Hope. Read scripture every day. Stay in communion with Him through prayer. Learn to observe evidence of His presence with you. Stay in love with God. Matthew?"

"Yes, sir?"

"Pray with your wife. Read scripture together. Send her reminders during the workday that you are thinking of her and praying for her. Pray about the therapy as well as your therapist. Pray about whether you should stay with her or find another. Be aware that you might be seeing your therapist for more than just getting help for yourself. Perhaps your faith can serve as a witness to her. Who knows?" Pastor squeezes her hands. "Maybe this is the very reason, just like Esther, for which you were created." He drops one of her hands and reaches for Matthew. "Let me pray for you."

After he finishes, Hope and Matthew join in with his 'Amen." He drops their hands and reaches for the check, but Matthew snatches it away. "No, sir," Matthew says, "we're getting this."

"May I leave the tip?"

Matthew jumps to his feet. "You already have. We can't thank you enough."

Hope buries her face in her former pastor's shoulder. She whispers, "Thank you. As painful as it may have been, it was so good to spend time with you." She breaks the embrace and takes his cool hands in hers. "You have given me encouragement."

"I will keep you in my prayers, dear child." Pastor Dave turns to Matthew and shakes his hand. "Don't hesitate to call on me again. God be with you both."

The next morning, Hope happily opens her front door to greet her friend, who carries a covered container of her homemade cinnamon rolls.

"Deb! How'd you know I was about to wither away?"

"I brought enough for all of you." Debbie turns her head from side to side as she follows Hope to her kitchen. "Appears like we have the house to ourselves, though. I guess Matthew and the kids are at the same place as my men?"

"Yep. Ball practice at the park district." Hope waves a hand toward the coffeemaker, which holds a nearly full, fragrant pot. "Get yourself a cup while I grab us plates."

Hope serves a cinnamon roll to each of them while Debbie pours dark coffee into a mug, steam rising from it. "We've sure got a pretty day out there today." Hope tosses the words over her shoulder. "Is it nice enough to sit out on the porch?"

"Oh, yeah." Debbie nods. "I'll bring your coffee."

As soon as they settle at the table on the porch facing the well-manicured lawn, Debbie jumps in as Hope takes a big bite. "So, tell me. How'd your visit with your old pastor go last night? I prayed all evening for you."

Hope washes down the cinnamon roll before recounting their dinner date from the previous evening. When she reaches the part where Pastor Dave tells her that her grandmother was found trapped under the boat, Debbie's eyes go wide, and her mouth drops open.

"But, she raised you to the surface! Hope, that's how you didn't drown."

"That's what I've always believed. But Pastor said it was impossible."

A silence falls between the friends as the meaning of this revelation settles on Debbie. A sense of peace envelops her as Hope directs her gaze to the swing set in the yard, which is draped beneath the old maple tree, the grass long worn away by her children's dragging feet. Birds chirp, and the hum of a mower from somewhere in the neighborhood serves as the backdrop.

"Hope?"

Debbie's eyes glimmer with wonder as Hope turns to face her. "Hope, do you suppose?"

"It's always possible, Deb. All I know is, I was lifted to the surface by warm hands." Hope inhales deeply through her nose. "I had always assumed those hands belonged to my Nana."

Debbie grins, showing her teeth, and her dimples deepen at the corners of her mouth. "Praise God. You are here." She lifts her coffee mug.

"Indeed." Hope copies her and they lightly tap the cups together. "I am."

They finish the sweet rolls and drink their coffee. Hope reports that after much prayer and contemplation, she made another appointment with Rachel, wanting to continue the therapy. Debbie's smile fades.

"I'm sorry I didn't warn you that she's not a believer." Debbie's brows draw together. "It didn't interfere with the things she helped me with."

Hope shakes her head. "Don't apologize. I sense that, now that Rachel knows, she will respect my beliefs."

Debbie's face brightens as she slightly tilts her head. "I suppose. And." She sighs. "You never know. If it's through your faith that the CBT helps, she may see how powerful hope in Christ is for the believer. If her heart is opened, that is."

Hope leans toward her friend. "You feel I should give her another chance, too?"

"Well." Debbie draws the word out. "If it helps, you just remember you got the referral from me."

"And if not?"

"Rachel, who?"

They both laugh. "Oh, hey." Debbie reaches for her smartphone. "I found something I think you might be interested in." After scrolling for a moment, she smiles. "Yeah, here it is. I did some digging. Did you know there is a program that offers swimming lessons for those afraid of water?"

"I know how to swim, Deb."

"Yeah, but do you? Swim?"

"No, but."

"Look." Debbie hands her phone to her friend.

"Oh, wow." Hope reads. "This sounds amazing. 'For adults who know they have a fear of water as well as for those who are adamant that they do not.' Interesting take."

"Not only that, but they offer lessons for adults

who have already learned to swim."

"Yeah, I see that."

"If you want a swim lesson buddy, I'm your girl."

Hope jerks her head toward her friend, eyes wide. "You? You're not afraid of water."

"Nope. But I don't know how to swim."

"What?" Hope sets the phone down, her mouth open. "Are you serious?"

"Absolutely." Debbie takes back her phone. "Situations were such that I never had the opportunity as a kid, and then, next thing I knew, I had kids of my own."

"And they swim."

"Sure, and I sit poolside and watch them with one eye and read with the other."

Hope gives a short laugh. "Okay, I'm in. You sign us up."

Debbie notes the time. "I gotta go. Oh, hey. Are you ready to teach us about John Wesley next Sunday?"

"Next Sunday, already? Oh, gee whiz!"

Debbie furrows her brows and points a finger at her. "You better be kidding. Mr. Hamilton concluded his study last Sunday."

Hope smiles at her friend. "I'm one hundred percent ready. This is gonna be the best one yet."

"Great. No fainting on us?"

"I will have the faith of a Wesley, my friend."

Debbie stands, gathering her things. "I take it JW got over his fear of death eventually?"

Hope grins. "You will have to wait until our next Sunday School study to find out."

Chapter Twenty-One

The angels of God have great power, in particular, over the human body... They may prevent our falling into many dangers... How many times have we been strangely and unaccountably preserved?
John Wesley

John Wesley
On the road to Bristol
23 January, 1748

It was only mid-morning, but John, as was his custom, had already filled the hours with business.

Out of bed at the fourth hour, he had spent his usual hour in private prayer and scripture reading before joining John Trembath for Bible study and breakfast. Now the pair sat perched on their saddles, their horses' hooves plodding along the packed dirt road as they traveled through the countryside. The creaking of leather saddles accentuated the clopping as their bodies swayed. Wesley much preferred the clean, crisp country air over the stench of the city. Even in the dead of winter, the country air had the ability to sweeten any mood.

However, despite the dreary day, it did not diminish John's hopeful determination. Typical January clouds obscured much of the sun, and a cool breeze brushed his hair against his neck, where he had neglected to turn up the collar of his greatcoat. He was uncertain about what awaited them in Deveral, their planned stop on the way to Bristol, but John was confident that, no matter what happened, God's presence would accompany them and God's kingdom would be advanced. The parish priests were known to send thugs to disrupt the Methodist outdoor prayer meetings, and he suspected this visit would be no different.

Trembath accompanied Wesley eagerly, though John suspected the young man was more interested in the societies of Bristol than in the people of Deveral and Bearfield. Trembath had a handsome face that bore no pockmarked scars and was framed by sandy blond hair. His mouth boasted all but one of his teeth, which Trembath reported losing after tripping down some stone steps. His smooth hands, free of calluses, held the reins. His clothing showed no signs of wear. To be honest, Wesley would have preferred to journey alone. However, while John Trembath showed promise, there was much for him to learn, and the Wesley brothers were the best teachers if the man were to become fully entrenched in the Methodist movement.

If John Wesley did think so himself.

That morning, they encountered several groups of fellow travelers on the road, which was not unusual for the well-traversed path. Trembath was careful to keep his horse behind Wesley's each time they met someone traveling from the opposite direction.

Wesley broke the silence that had settled between them. "You have not yet visited the societies in Bristol, have you?"

"No, I have not. That's why I was eager to accompany you this time. The colliers are a peculiar people, aren't they?"

"Different from what you may have been raised with. But their conditions make them ever so more yearning for the good news of Christ. Remember, Christ came to proclaim good news to the poor. As his disciples, we must do the same."

"But aren't they, well, terribly coarse?"

John Wesley brought his horse to a stop, forcing Trembath do the same. He stared intently into the young man's green eyes.

"What happens," Wesley asked, "when metal is forged in fire and beaten on the anvil?"

Trembath opened his mouth but quickly closed it without answering.

"There are no soft angles on such a sword, John Trembath. Hard conditions work like the refiner's fire and hammer onto the souls of men, creating good weapons in the war against evil."

Wesley urged his horse onward, and the two travelers lapsed into a thoughtful silence.

The wind picked up, and Wesley turned the collar of his coat close to his neck. The weather had been warmer than usual for the past few days, so he was unprepared for the chill as the breeze tugged at him. He silently thanked the Lord for the coat and the riding gloves while holding the reins loosely in his hands.

The sound of trickling water signaled that they were nearing the river. The scent in the air changed subtly, blending the unique river smell with that of the open countryside. John pulled up and leaned toward Trembath, who turned to him with a question in his eyes.

Wesley nodded forward. "There's a land bridge ahead. The road passes through it, but narrows considerably, and the bridge is long enough that if we meet anyone coming the other way, it can be dangerous. Be cautious and keep watch."

Trembath nodded in understanding, and they moved forward, entering the bridge. Deveral lay close beyond it, and Wesley rehearsed a part of the sermon he had prepared to deliver there. His eyes were fixed on the back of his horse's head, whose mane glistened and shook with every step.

They were already halfway across the bridge when Trembath's voice broke his reverie. "Mr. Wesley, shall we turn back?"

John raised his head. Up ahead, two oxen were hitched to a wagon, and the single driver wore a weathered greatcoat and concern on his face. There was no room for even a single horse to pass the wagon without one of them being driven off the road. Wesley halted.

What to do?

Look down.

A narrow strip of land stretched between the road and the rugged bank of the river on either side of the bridge. There was barely enough room for those on horseback to pass in single file, accommodating the wide girth of the wagon.

John eased his horse onto the narrow strip of land. Large, irregular rocks covered the riverbank. His horse snorted, and John sensed its unease. The wagon approached, with Trembath following close behind him.

Several things happened simultaneously. Another gust of cold wind blew against them from across the river. The oxen trudged alongside them when John's horse whinnied and reared, edging toward the perilous rocky bank. Trembath's horse snorted and tossed its head. As it did, the bit on its bridle caught a button on Wesley's greatcoat and yanked him from his ride.

The wind ceased. Time stood still. In slow motion, Wesley fell. The cold air surged between him and his horse. But then, something like warm hands cradled him and laid him gently on the ground, right on the narrow strip of land. A few inches to one side, his body would have smashed against the rocks. A few inches the other way, the wagon wheels creaked past his head.

John lay on his back, staring at the sky above. A tiny beam of sunlight broke through the clouds and illuminated the pair. The eternity of those few moments passed before Trembath exclaimed. "Mr. Wesley, are you harmed? Can you move?"

The wagon had creaked by. The horses stood calmly, one positioned directly behind him and the other right in front of him. They had not trampled him.

Astonished, Wesley sat upright. "I am well." He stood and brushed his greatcoat with both hands. He grasped his horse's reins, whispered soothing sounds in its ear, and then remounted. Returning to the road, he turned to Trembath, whose mouth still hung open.

Praise God. Now, come on, Mr. Trembath. We'll still make it to Deveral with plenty of time to spare.

"What exactly occurred back there?"

Wesley and Trembath watered their horses as soon as they entered the hamlet of Deveral. John wished he had some kind of treat for both of their horses, a thank-you gift for not trampling him. However, his pockets were empty of anything adequate.

"Mr. Wesley?"

Trembath placed a hand on his arm. John regarded him. "You mean the fall. Of course, it was miraculous."

"Yes! It could have ended you in any number of ways." Trembath's eyes blazed with passion. "Surely, God is with you."

If they weren't heading to Bearfield after this, John would remove the saddles, blankets, and their gear and brush down the horses. But if what he was forewarned about happened, there might be a need for a quick escape from Deveral.

"A few inches one way or the other, you may have been killed."

"That possibility occurred to me as well."

"And the horses. One moment, they panicked, snickering, and rearing, but then a moment later, they stood calm. Like good soldiers. What do you suppose?"

It was Wesley's turn to lay a hand on Trembath's arm. "After so many times of being rescued by God's angels, you get used to it." He removed his hand and took the reins. Turning, he led his horse away from the water trough. "Now, we must join our people. We are to congregate in the square."

His mouth agape, Trembath shook his head. "How can you be so nonchalant about this? I don't understand."

"I assure you, I do not take the protection of heaven for granted. The evidence of His grace abounds. And if my opponents were correct and I am of the devil, would my crushed and broken body be lying on that bridge right this moment? Of course, they may claim that the devil and his angels preserve their own, as well." Wesley shrugged as they neared the neighborhood square. "I suggest that it depends entirely on one's point of view." He leaned toward his companion. "Am I a disciple of Christ or a disciple of Satan?"

After hitching their horses, Wesley noted around twenty folks already gathered. Several vendors had their wares displayed, and a handful of customers stood before them. Wesley felt warmth as he was greeted by several of the men awaiting their arrival, and he called them by name before introducing John Trembath to them.

The crowd increased. The hamlet already had a couple of class meeting groups, each consisting of about ten people. The sole objective of the meetings was to nurture the spiritual growth of each believer. They provided someone to learn from, someone to encourage, and someone to hold them accountable.

The episode on the bridge weighed heavily on Wesley's mind as he began his sermon. He had prepared it earlier in the week, with no knowledge of the impending experience of yet another miraculous rescue at the hands of his guardian angels.

"The scripture today is from Saint Paul's second letter to the Corinthians."

John Trembath opened his Bible and read.

"'Would to God ye could bear with me a little in my folly: and indeed bear with me. For I am jealous over you with godly jealousy: for I have espoused you to one husband that I may present you as a chaste virgin to Christ. But I fear, lest by any means, as the serpent beguiled Eve through his subtilty, so your minds be corrupted from the simplicity that is in Christ.'"

"Kindly skip ahead to verse nineteen, Mr. Trembath."

"Certainly, sir." Using his forefinger, he skimmed to the prescribed verse. "'For ye suffer fools gladly, seeing ye yourselves are wise. For ye suffer, if a man bring you into bondage, if a man devour you, if a man take from you, if a man exalt himself, if a man smite you on the face. I speak as concerning reproach, as though we had been weak. Howbeit, whereinsoever any is bold (I speak foolishly), I am bold also.'"

The crowd had grown. Neighbors joined the society members. The vendors and their customers all turned to listen. For some, hearing the Word of God preached outdoors, especially outside the walls of the church, was a new experience—something that simply wasn't done.

"Are they Hebrews? So am I. Are they Israelites? So am I. Are they the seed of Abraham? So am I. Are they ministers of Christ (I speak as a fool)? I am more; in labours more abundant, in stripes above measure, in prisons more frequent, in deaths oft."

A man on horseback sauntered into the square. Based on his attire, John assumed he was the Gwinear-Gwinthian parish priest. He wore his pious garb and a smirk on his face.

"Of the Jews, five times I received forty stripes

save one. Thrice was I beaten with rods, once was I stoned, thrice I suffered a shipwreck, a night and a day I have been in the deep; In journeyings often, in perils of waters, in perils of robbers, in perils by mine own countrymen."

The jarring shouts of the mob reached their ears. Even Trembath paused to follow their approach. Amid their cries, cowbells and chains clanked and clattered. Mobs often brought whatever they could grab to try to drown him out.

"Go on." Wesley spoke to Trembath, not under his breath, but with a clear, calm voice, and loud enough that the parish priest's smile began to fade.

"Mine own countrymen," Trembath repeated. "In perils by the heathen, in perils in the city, in perils in the wilderness, in perils in the sea, in perils among false brethren." Trembath dared a glance toward the priest himself before resuming. "In weariness and painfulness, in watchings often, in hunger and thirst, in fastings often, in cold and nakedness. Besides those things which that are without, that which cometh upon me daily, the care of all the churches. Who is weak, and I am not weak? Who is offended, and I burn not?"

Trembath closed his Bible and turned to John Wesley. The mob stood at the far edge of the square, still shouting and banging on pots, rattling their chains and cowbells. John spread his hands and began to speak.

"When Saint Paul wrote in his letter to the Romans that we glory in tribulations also, knowing that tribulations worketh patience, and patience, experience, and experience, hope, he knew of what he spoke."

The mob moved in closer, their noise growing

louder. However, John continued to preach, and those around him heard every word.

"But did not our Lord Jesus Christ say, in his sermon on the mount, 'Blessed are they which are persecuted for righteousness' sake: for theirs is the kingdom of heaven'? 'Blessed are ye, when men shall revile you and persecute you.'"

Turn your head to the left.

John did not hesitate. Without pausing in his speech, he turned to his left. The moment he did, a large rock whooshed past his ear, sending a breeze through his hair.

"'And shall say all manner of evil against you.'"

"Take that, you son of the devil!" Rocks and rotten eggs flew through the air. Trembath crouched behind Wesley, who kept preaching, his voice steady and unwavering.

"'Falsely, for my sake.'" Wesley made eye contact with the parish priest, who sat, statue-like, on his mount, all mirth gone from his countenance. "'Rejoice,'" Wesley thundered, "'and be exceedingly glad: for great is your reward in heaven: for so persecuted they the prophets which were before you.'"

John's collar was turned up against the cold Bristol night air as he walked to the rowhouse that his brother Charles was renting.

While it was well past sunset, there was still quite a bit of foot and horse traffic on the busy city street. John tried the latch, and the door opened. Unlocked. He shook his head as he stepped into the dark entryway.

"Charles?" His voice echoed.

A chair scraped nearby, and footsteps echoed as his brother emerged from his study on John's right.

"Jack? I wasn't expecting you until breakfast." Charles wiped his inky fingertips with a handkerchief. "Well, make yourself at home."

"I dropped off Trembath at Kingswood. He is staying in the room there and will join us on the morrow. May I stay with you while we're in Bristol?" John dropped his bag on the floor, then slipped off his greatcoat and hung it on a peg near the door. "Your house smells of cabbage."

Charles grinned at him. "Of course, you're always welcome. Can I get you something to drink? You sound a bit hoarse. Been doing a lot of talking, I presume."

"Only some water, if you will."

"Go sit by the fire and warm yourself in the parlor. I'll be right there."

John stepped into the room to his left. The fire blazed perfectly, with little tendrils of smoke swirling above the flames as they curled up the chimney. The window facing the street had its curtains drawn, which helped to retain the heat. Two chairs stood near the fireplace, facing one another, as if Charles anticipated the company of just one more guest. John sat down and rubbed his hands together to get the blood flowing.

Charles entered the room carrying a tray with two mugs and a pitcher. He set the tray on a low table nearby and served his brother before serving himself. John waited until Charles was seated across from him.

I'm still surprised you rented a place on such a busy street. I thought you'd prefer someplace quieter for your writing.

Charles sipped his water. "I'm not that distracted

by the noise. Not for the price, anyway." He placed his cup on the floor, away from the fire. "How did Deveral turn out? As predicted?"

The firelight cast a warm glow around Charles's face. Behind him, shadows danced on the wall. The odors of coal, wood, and remnants of the evening meal mingled in the air. John held his mug with both hands.

"Exactly as I was warned. The parish priest had his purchased mob, liquored them up, and loaded them with their usual ammunition."

Charles studied his fingers for any further ink. "Well, the violence isn't something we've never faced before. I'd be disappointed if no mob or gang were sent to try to stop us or drown us out." Charles' handsome face wore a sideways grin, and his eyes danced with devilish glee. "It's how we know that what we have to say is dangerous to their devilish ways." He clasped his hands together and studied his brother across from him. "Something else happened, though, didn't it? Something you're not telling me."

John contemplated the crackling fire, hesitant to bring up the weighty subject that sat heavy on his heart, yet longing for his brother's thoughts. The entire house around him stilled as if it were taking a breath.

"What do you think Milton meant when he wrote of the 'millions of spiritual creatures'? Is there more unseen than seen, do you believe?"

Charles inhaled audibly, pausing before responding. "Is that a rhetorical question, Jack? I never know with you."

John turned his gaze back to his brother. Apart from their mother, Charles's opinions and thoughts meant the most to him. This younger brother, who almost wasn't, was an absolute gift from God.

"No," John answered. "I'm asking a genuine question. What are your beliefs about the many different spiritual beings that we cannot see but experience in various ways?"

Charles's eyes flicked between John's two, unable to settle on just one. He leaned closer and uttered a harshly whispered response. "What happened, Jack? Tell me every detail."

John took a long drink from his water before setting it on the floor as well. Then he met his brother's eyes and shared the story of the incident on the Develar long bridge. After explaining how he remounted his horse and stepped back onto the road, he paused.

Charles sat back and rested his arms on the arms of his chair. He blew out an exhale as if he had been holding his breath throughout John's story. "Did you hit your head? Maybe after your horse reared?"

"No. My noggin was unharmed even as I landed. Correction. I didn't land. When my body was laid on the ground."

Charles closed his eyes. "That could have gone wrong for you in so many ways."

"Yes. I most definitely understand that."

Charles's eyes flew back open. "Jack, how many times in your life might you have died? Beginning with the fire in the rectory?"

"Actually, one might consider the fact that either of us, any of us brothers and sisters, survived to adulthood something of a miracle."

"Yes, but beyond that. Children don't survive house fires at night."

"We were all spared at sea."

"We have had stones thrown at us, we have been knocked down in the streets, we have had bulls loosed on us."

"I had a warning at Develar, too." John related hearing a voice in his head and how a stone flew past, nearly grazing his head. "It would have hit me square in the forehead."

Charles scoots back in his chair and stands. "This goes beyond the common 'slings and arrows' of common misfortune. All these violent acts are intended to kill you, to silence you." He gesticulated. "The very hand of God protects you."

John glanced up at his brother. "And you."

Charles shook his head. "Well, yes, but I have yet to be snatched out of the air when thrown from a horse and laid out on the ground as if with a mother's arms." He thrust a hand toward John. "But you? In the same twenty-four hours, your guardian angel worked a full shift, as if he were a Bristol collier."

John grinned. "That's a mental picture that I will not soon lose. Sit, Charles. Tell me what you believe. About guardian angels, and spirits in general."

Charles sat on the edge of his seat. "Well, we know we all have them. In the gospel of Saint Matthew, our Lord is recorded as relating that fact."

"Yes," John quoted. "Take heed that ye despise not one of these little ones, for I say unto you that in heaven their angels do always behold the face of my Father."

"One must reason that angels are assigned to them. And to us."

"And all the experiences of Saint Paul, and Saint Peter, being ministered by angels."

"We know guardian angels are different from messenger angels."

"Agreed. And they operate differently from the Holy Ghost, who gives us spiritual direction. These guardians seem to be exactly that. Physical bodyguards."

"Yes, they protect us from physical threats. But I also believe there must be other guardians to protect us from spiritual harm."

"A host of angels. Or at least a goodly group of spirits assigned to us."

"We have been given the power to rebuke the evil spirits. What about ghosts?"

Charles huffed. "We experienced such an entity at the Rectory. It was impossible not to acknowledge that creature. I can't believe Father took that long to acknowledge it and cast it out." Charles rose once again. "Wait here." He began to walk away, then turned back to John. "Can you read with only the light from the fire?"

John studied his hands. The fire had died down too much. "No, I don't believe so."

"Then follow me into my study. We need to consult the Word."

Charles's study had sufficient candle and lamp light for both reading and writing. The brothers each held a Bible in their hands.

"On the count of three," John said. "One, two, three."

They opened their Bibles. John's eyes landed on Saint Paul's second letter to the Corinthians. "Hmph."

"What do you have?" Charles asked.

"Second Corinthians."

"Me too. My eyes fell on chapter four."

John's mouth dropped open. "So did mine. What verse did you see first?"

"Eight and nine. 'We are troubled on every side, yet not distressed, we are perplexed but not in despair, persecuted but not forsaken; cast down but not destroyed.' You?"

John wet his lips before reading. "Eighteen. 'While we look not at the things which are seen, but at the things—" Charles joined him—"which are not seen."

John closed his Bible and met his brother's intense scrutiny. "We need to pray."

Charles placed his closed Bible on his desk and joined him as they knelt on the chilly floor.

John thanked God for their many blessings, recalling as many as came to his mind. He expressed gratitude for the gift of his son, Jesus, and for the forgiveness of their sins and the sins of the world. He concluded with one of the short prayers used in the church liturgy. "O everlasting God, who hast ordained and constituted the services of angels and men in a wonderful manner, grant that as thy holy angels always do thee service in heaven, so by thy appointment, they may succor and defend us on earth, through Jesus Christ our Lord."

After they stood up, Charles noted the time. "Four o'clock will arrive quickly, Jack. Best get some rest, while you can. I'll be upstairs shortly."

John made his way to the stairway, his steps cautious in the dark where the lamp light barely reached. When he turned at the landing, he entered an area so cold it made him pause. However, as quickly as he had walked into it, warmth radiated around him, as if the entity had been banished to the dark, chilly streets of Bristol.

Chapter Twenty-Two

Be still, and know that I am God: I will be exalted among the heathen, I will be exalted in the earth. The LORD *of hosts is with us; the God of Jacob is our refuge.*
Psalm 46:10–11

Hope
Webster Groves, Missouri
Two weeks later

It was a beautiful June morning, and Hope's mood mirrored the weather: sunny and expectant.

The drive to their new swim class took a couple of hours, but she and Debbie believed that the driving time would boost their confidence, and the journey home would provide an excellent opportunity to evaluate the experience of the class. Plus, Hope enjoys Debbie's company more and more, especially since they had both incorporated morning prayer and Bible study into their lives. Matthew had taken Pastor Dave's advice and texted her prayers every workday. She and Matthew prayed together each night before bedtime. Hope shared with Debbie how her daily walk with the Lord was enhancing not only her marriage but also her faith.

After Debbie enters the parking lot and glides into a spot, Hope unbuckles her seatbelt. Just as she reaches for the door handle, Debbie stops her.

"Hold up there, Eager Beaver. Mind if I pray over us?"

Hope settles back in the passenger seat. "Please."

Debbie grasps Hope's hand. "Lord, we thank you so much for today and for bringing us here. Please be with us as we begin this adventure. Grant us your peace. In Jesus's name, amen."

"Amen. Now, can we go in?"

"Sheesh, you're more excited than I expected." Debbie laughs as she opens the driver's door.

They grab their bags containing their swimsuits and flip-flops from the back seats and enter the brick building. A sheet of paper taped to the double glass doors informs them they are in the right place. Hope can't shake the feeling that she is entering a time portal. The thick-paned windows frame pale green, glossy-painted brick walls, and their footsteps echo as they walk on the tan floor tiles, accented with dark brown squares. "You suppose this used to be a YMCA or something?"

Debbie sniffs the air. "I can definitely smell the pool." When the hallway breaks off in a T, she points to their right. "My nose says the chlorine is down this way."

Midway down the hallway, a silver-haired woman sits at a table with a few papers scattered before her. "Good morning, ladies! My name is Marjie." She points to the "Hello! My name is" sticker on her left chest. "This is the Fearless Water introduction class. May I have your names, please?" After crossing off their names from what Hope notices is a short list, Marjie writes their names on similar-looking name badges and steps back from the table to stand. "The classroom is right inside here."

Hope receives the name badge but tilts her head. "Not the dressing room?"

Marjie smiles, her dimples deepening in the soft wrinkles around her mouth. "The dressing room is later. You'll be chomping at the bit by the time you get there." She points to a table along one wall of the room, filled with refreshments. "Help yourself to water, tea, or soda. Class will start soon."

Hope and Debbie step further into the classroom, where school desks, the kind she hadn't seen since college, are arranged facing a large dry-erase board. A tall, dark young man is sorting through papers at a table in the front, and there are already a few others seated in the front row. The man raises his gaze and smiles at them.

"Ladies, come on in. We'll get started here in a few minutes." He indicates near the front rows. "Sit close, if you don't mind."

Debbie leans into Hope, speaking aside. "Don't mind having to look at that, if I may say so."

"Oh, Deb!"

Chuckling, Hope slips into a desk in the second row. "This will give you a good vantage point."

Only five more people drift in before the instructor introduces himself as D'Wayne and writes his name on the whiteboard. His voice is warm and calm, as are his dark brown eyes.

"While some people know they have a fear of the water, others may not be aware. If you are not at peace, if you are *uncomfortable* at any point in the water, this class is for you."

He surveys the class, making eye contact with each of them. "Let me make this clear: you were not born with this fear. Something happened to cause that fear, something that made you feel out of control, that caused you to learn that fear. The brain, complex and wonderful as it is, is designed to learn. It cannot unlearn."

"So, you are here to learn something new." Their instructor pauses and meets Hope's eyes. "Are you ready to learn something new? Are you ready to be at peace in the water?"

Hope's mouth drops open. Debbie reaches over and touches her arm. Hope cannot look away from the man. This is an absolute answer to prayer. Thank you, Jesus.

"The key to learning to swim is not found in having the right techniques, the correct strokes, kicking versus pulling. These skills have their places, of course, but the true goal is comfort, feeling in control, and having fun doing it."

He looks away at another student, and Hope releases her breath. She remembers how much fun she had taking swim lessons at the Y as a child. She took to swimming naturally. Back then, she loved how being in the water made her feel. She sorely misses that feeling. Where did that little girl go?

"Swimming technique is meaningless if you cannot feel what is happening in the water. You must first learn how to feel."

D'Wayne turns to the dry-erase board and, grabbing a marker, draws five stick figure pictures surrounded in various ways by an oval. He caps the marker before turning back to the class.

"We must first have a basic understanding of ourselves. We are not bodies. We are spirits that have bodies. You must have a solid understanding of this fact before we can go any further."

From deep within her chest, Hope feels a growing warmth.

"Your body does not control you. *You* control your body."

The warmth in Hope's chest spreads.

"Now, hear this." D'Wayne gazes out beyond them as if he is staring at something or someone on the back wall of the room. "You must be present if you hope to learn to swim."

For the next hour, the man explains the illustrations. Hope has to admit that most of the time, she is not present in her body. Her mind is almost always elsewhere—with her husband at work or in his car on the drive home, with her children at school, or even on a ship in the Atlantic Ocean in 1736 with John and Charles Wesley. She acknowledges that if her mind was elsewhere when she stepped ever so gingerly into that hotel pool a few weeks ago, she did not feel in control.

"How many of you have ever panicked?" D'Wayne raises his hand, along with much of the class. "Panic happens when our spirit is not grounded in its body. The spirit is not recognizing the peace and calm we should feel within ourselves. Let's learn now about our internal speed and how to slow it down."

During the break, Debbie and Hope rush to the restroom.

"Isn't this amazing?" Debbie dries her hands after washing.

"Who knew that learning to swim could be a spiritual practice?" Hope shakes her head. "You know, before the accident, I wanted to be a lifeguard when I was old enough." Hope checks her reflection in the mirror. She almost sees her twelve-year-old self gazing back at her. "I think God wants me in this class." Hope turns to her friend.

Debbie's bright eyes swim. She nods. "Me too, Hope. Me too."

After another hour of instruction, during which they learned to be aware of their bodies' sensations, D'Wayne clasps his hands toward them. "So. Who is ready to get in the water?"

Hope raises her hand eagerly, shouting along with the rest of the class. She can't wait to put on her suit and slip into the warm water. She, Debbie, and five other women giggle as they rush out of the women's locker room to join the men. They stand closely together, surrounding D'Wayne as he continues.

"I want you all to go at your own pace. Start slow and remain in control. If you feel yourself slipping out of drawing number one, at any point, you should go back to where you are comfortable again."

We have the water temperature around 93 degrees. This is warmer than most pools. Fear is cold, and we don't want you to feel cold. If you choose to practice in a cooler pool, you might consider getting a wetsuit for that purpose. Now, I want you to ease into the water in whatever way you feel most comfortable.

Then observe. Note your surroundings and your feelings. Pay attention to how your body feels, your internal speed, and your heart rate. And, guys?" He grins and spreads his hands wide. "Have fun!

Hope and Debbie wait as the others step into the pool. Hope peers into the water, which is tinted by the blue paint of the pool. She breathes in the chlorine-scented air emanating from the room and smiles. She focuses on the feel of the concrete beneath her feet as she confidently steps onto the pool steps. One step at a time, she inhales through her nose and exhales through her mouth. As she ventures further in, Hope feels the warm water enveloping her, and she becomes aware of every inch of her body as she descends a little deeper. The water reaches her hips, and she reaches down to swirl her hands through it. The warmth in her chest returns, and she senses a whisper in her ears.

"Hello, water," Hope murmurs. She settles into a space of peace.

Hope loses track of time. Her fingers are wrinkled when their instructor encourages them to exit the pool. She grins at him as she wraps herself in a warm towel. Debbie joins her as D'Wayne turns to both of them.

"So," he says, "what do you think?"

Hope brushes some hair back from her eye and can't stop grinning. "When's the next class?"

The following week

"I was very encouraged when you called to schedule, Hope."

Hope is once again seated across the coffee table

from Rachel. She sweeps her gaze around the room. Sunlight streams through the closed mini-blinds at the window, illuminating the space sufficiently that the floor lamps are unnecessary. Something feels different, but she can't put her finger on it. The diffuser releases a continuous mist, but without any new scent. The decor remains unchanged. Even the ticking clock continues its familiar beat.

She turns her attention back to Rachel. Maybe she cut her hair. But no, she appears no different. She might even be wearing the same clothes she had on the last time Hope was here. Same chewed pencil, same legal pad.

Maybe the difference isn't Rachel or her office. *Maybe the thing that has changed is me.*

"I've had some, well, interesting breakthroughs," Hope says. "I'd like your take on them. And then I have some specific advice I would like from you."

"This sounds interesting." Hope observes a flicker of curiosity in the therapist's eyes. "Start wherever you prefer, Hope."

"Do you have any water? I'm afraid I hurried here without grabbing any, and I'm a bit dry."

Rachel returns with a disposable cup filled with chilled water, which Hope gladly accepts. After half-draining the drink, she sets it on the coffee table. "Thanks, that helps." She takes a deep breath. "This may take a bit, so I hope we don't run out of time."

Rachel remains silent but gestures to Hope with her pencil-holding hand to continue.

"My husband and I resolved to consult with my old pastor, the one who knew me when I was young, during the accident, and after. I wanted his opinion of my, well, my issues, the dreams, my diagnosis. Things like that."

Rachel nods, but her eyes are on her legal pad as she jots down a few words.

"I learned something very important. Well, a couple of things. I told him about the dreams. Then I told him how preparing the Sunday School lesson about Wesley brought out the PTSD, as you explained it to me."

"Seems like merely thinking about storms on bodies of water is definitely one of your triggers."

"That's right. Then Matthew explained to him that I blame myself for Nana's death."

Rachel tilts her head. "Did you tell me about that?"

Hope shakes her head. "I don't think so. I have been so ashamed."

Rachel silently edges the tissue box closer to her, but Hope doesn't reach for it.

"You see, I was thirteen. I was only starting to notice boys. I had a cute swimsuit, and I wanted to show it off," Hope shrugs. "You know."

Rachel smiles with encouragement.

"The last thing I wanted, or thought I needed, was a life jacket. So, I laid out on the front of the boat, sunning. Until there was no sun. The storm came on fast. I—I was in the water before I became aware of what had happened."

"I see. Since you didn't put on a life jacket—"

"It was my fault Nana died trying to save me. Or, that's what I have always believed."

"How old were you when your parents died, Hope?"

"Oh, I was super young. Not quite three."

"Do you have any memory of them?"

Hope closes her eyes. She has one very brief, hazy picture in her head. "I remember being rocked, looking up at my mom's face." Hope opens her eyes. "But that's all I have."

Rachel scribbles some more.

Hope resumes. "Pastor Dave, however, assured me of two very important things. One." Hope indicates with an index finger. "Even if I'd worn a life jacket, Nana would have jumped in after me. He said that it was her maternal instinct to do so. But most importantly, two." The second finger joined the first. "Nana got disoriented in the water. She didn't wear a life jacket, either. She wasn't the best swimmer. And, she was found trapped under the boat. The same people who grabbed me out of the water observed the entire thing."

Rachel furrows her brows. "She jumped in but got trapped under the boat?"

"Yes."

"After she brought you to the surface."

Hope shakes her head. "No. Not according to first-hand witnesses."

"Then who?" Rachel's frown deepens.

"That's the million-dollar question, now, isn't it?" Hope reaches for her water and finishes it off.

"Someone else must have—"

"There was no one else. It all happened over a very short period of time. A huge wave came along as Nana throttled down the boat, and I was thrown pretty far. Nana cut the engine and jumped into the lake after me. I came to the surface." Hope peers into Rachel's eyes. "Nana did not."

"I see. You must have imagined being raised to the surface."

Hope again shakes her head. "I remember very clearly the voice in my head, and I distinctly remember the warm hands."

"Hope, that's impossible."

Hope smiles. "Yet, here I am."

"Okay, well, yes. So you are."

Hope takes a deep breath. "Well, that has been a huge relief. I mean, the end result is still the same. My beloved grandmother died, leaving me and Papa with only each other. But now I know."

"And that has helped you?"

"Tremendously. Then, Debbie found a special swim class designed for adults who are afraid of deep water. We've gone to five lessons together so far, and it's been great. Our instructor taught us how to be aware of our bodies. Right now, I'm mindful of my feet. I feel them in my shoes. They are both flat on the floor."

The corners of Rachel's mouth turn up. "I think I've heard something about this program. Isn't it spiritually based?"

"Well, yes and no. The method is based on the understanding that we are spirits, inhabiting a body. But it's not necessarily faith-based." Hope searches Rachel's face before she continues. "It's absolutely amazing. I need to get you the information, as it might be helpful if you had any other clients with deep water-associated fears or trauma."

"I appreciate that." Rachel glances at the clock. "There was some advice you wanted from me?"

"Yes. Well, Matthew and I believe we might be able to incorporate CBT with my newly regained comfort in water. While warm water, which is warmer than pools are typically kept, is best for the classes, I think I'm ready to challenge myself with some significant triggers. What would you suggest?"

Rachel gave a short laugh. "Well, I don't think you're ready to take a ski boat out on a lake during a thunderstorm. But." She doodles a bit on her paper as she thinks. "Someplace with a lot of splashing, some deeper water. Deep enough to truly swim." Her head tips up abruptly. "Do you want another family outing?"

Hope smiles. "I'd love that."

"How about an indoor water park? Complete with various water slides and a wave pool. Even a lazy river when you're exhausted from splashing fun. How does that sound?"

"That sounds perfect!"

"There's one at the resort in the city. Just far enough away, your kids will feel like you're taking a mini-vacation."

"That's a great idea." Hope removes her checkbook from her purse and writes out a check. Handing it to Rachel, she remarks. "Let me call you and let you know how it goes. If all goes well, I may not need another session. At least, not too soon. You're a gem, Rachel. Thank you so much."

Hope walks around the table and brings her therapist in for a hug.

"I'll give you a call." Hope chuckles to herself at the look on Rachel's face as she departs.

Chapter Twenty-Three

And all they in the synagogue, when they heard
these things, were filled with wrath, and rose up, and
thrust him out of the city, and led him unto the brow of
the hill whereon their city was built, that they might
cast him down headlong. But he, passing through the
midst of them, went his way.
Luke 4:28–30

John Wesley
Falmouth, Cornwall, England
July, 1745

John hesitated only momentarily before knocking on the outer door of the Beckwith home.

"Welcome, Reverend Wesley. The mistress and her daughter are expecting you."

He stepped into the home's entryway and followed the maid through the inner door into the sitting room. Widow Beckwith had summoned John to Falmouth for a visit. Reports of disturbances among the townsfolk had reached him, as they were upset about the privately held Methodist class meetings in town.

Threats of violence had caused a great deal of caution. There was hesitancy to attend worship on Sunday mornings for fear of being accosted or prevented from entering the churches. Therefore, John had brought along the elements so they might celebrate the Lord's communion in the safety of their home.

"Reverend Wesley, it has been awful." Mrs. Beckwith sat, her back straight, her hands folded in her lap. "My daughter and I fear for our lives. Why, only last week, a crowd attacked the home of the Snowdons while they held a class meeting, broke out the windows, and set the porch afire."

Mrs. Beckwith's daughter leaned toward him with her hands clasped. "Another group of us was attacked while walking together down the street, pelted with rocks and rotten eggs!"

John nodded, his mouth grim. "So persecuted they the prophets which were before you. Did not Saint Paul and Silas rejoice when they were beaten and imprisoned?"

"Yes, but they were men, sir," her daughter continued. "This rabble cares not whether their victims are men, women, or children!"

"Do you know these persecutors?" John asked the young lady's mother, fully aware that she had lived in the town her entire life.

"Yes, of course," Mrs. Beckwith answered. "They are townsfolk."

"Your neighbors." John didn't frame it as a question.

"Correct."

"And what did the Lord tell us about how we should treat our neighbors?"

The house was quiet, as if anticipating something. The large clock in the sitting room clunked while the pendulum swung back and forth. The mid-afternoon sun poured through the windows onto the three of them.

John waited. The fear of the women was evident to him. He dared not reassure them that they wouldn't continue facing persecution. His job was to teach them to rely on the Holy Ghost for strength in times of persecution. He redirected his question. "What did the Lord say was the greatest commandment?"

Mrs. Beckwith's daughter answered. "To love the Lord our God with all our heart, with all our souls, and with all our minds."

"Very good. And the second?" John turned to Mrs. Beckwith.

She dropped her chin and regarded her hands. "To love thy neighbor as thyself."

"Exactly right."

"But how does one..." Mrs. Beckwith frowned. "What is that I hear?"

Distant shouts fell on John's ears, and he rose.

Sir! Reverend Wesley." The maid hurried into the room, clutching her skirts. "Do you hear them? What shall we do?"

To the maid, he said, "I suggest you lock the doors, Miss." He then turned to Mrs. Beckwith and her daughter. "Ladies, perhaps we should move away from the windows."

The daughter sprang to her feet. "Oh, Mother! Let's hurry upstairs. Surely, they are here to destroy us."

Even as the shouts closed in, the words remained indistinct. John couldn't help but picture the rectory fire, a vivid memory from his childhood. He imagined a group marching toward the house, brandishing torches. "No," he said, "perhaps the pantry is safer. It is an inner room."

"How can you be so calm, Reverend Wesley?" Mrs. Beckwith's hands trembled as her daughter guided her toward the pantry on the main floor.

"Because God is with me, madam, as He is with you."

John was about to say more when there was a loud pounding at the front door. The demand came through loud and clear.

"Open up! Bring out the Methodist!"

Wesley ushered the ladies into the pantry. Before closing the door, he admonished them, saying, "Do not open this door until there is silence."

At the moment he turned from the pantry door, there was a loud boom of something slamming against the outer door. A battering ram? The shouting grew louder now, with repeated requests to "send out the Methodist."

The maid screamed. "They're busting down the door, sir. Make them stop!"

"Miss, perhaps you should join the ladies in the pantry." The words had barely left his mouth when, with a loud crash, the outer door slammed against the entryway floor. A window shattered in the sitting room, and the clamor of the murderous crowd grew to a deafening roar.

"We know you are in there." The man's voice was close, directly on the other side of the inner door. "If you don't come out, we'll drag you out."

Wesley stood, feet planted in the hallway before

the inner door, remaining silent.

"Avast lads, avast!"

The hinges broke, and the inner door crashed down at John's feet. Before him stood a gang of muscular sailors, their faces flushed and their eyes seething. Behind them was a crowd of men, some wielding clubs, others holding torches. All wore hatred in their eyes.

A peace filled him. The presence of the Holy Ghost was with him, and he was flooded with knowledge about what he was to do. He splayed his palms forward and stepped toward them. "Here I am." He locked eyes with one of the sailors. "What harm have I done you?" He turned his attention to another. "Or to you?" He lifted his eyes beyond them. "Or to any of you?" He lowered his hands to his side and strode through the now-quiet crowd.

Wesley peered at all the red, angry faces as much as he could, repeatedly asking, "Have I caused you any harm?" He continued this way until he stood in the center of them, in the street.

He addressed those surrounding him. "Neighbors, countrymen." The words came to him, words he was to say. "Do you desire to hear me speak?"

"Yes." The answer was soft, coming from a man right next to him.

"Yes!" came another.

Then the crowd cried out as one. "Yes, speak! He shall speak."

And speak he did.

John preached as the crowd listened intently. There was no heckling, no derision, and no rocks thrown. Once he concluded, the audience dispersed one by one. He remained unscathed, standing alone in the middle of the street.

Chapter Twenty-Four

But God hath not given us the spirit of fear; but of power, and of love, and of a sound mind.
2 Timothy 1:7

Hope
The following week

Matthew took a few days off in the middle of the week after Hope's last therapy session. It was easier to find an available room at the Big Bear Resort, which indeed features a large indoor water park, just as Rachel had promised. Even at the late hour the Gerard family arrived at the resort, children of all ages chased one another while frantic parents tried to herd them one way or another.

They had arrived late the night before, too late for Eric and Samantha to change into their swimsuits and enjoy the last hour at the water park before it closed. Their fallen faces clearly displayed their disappointment, prompting Hope and Matthew to promise that they'd be the first people there in the morning when the water park opened.

Matthew had brought donuts, coffee, and milk up to the room for breakfast, which the kids wolfed down while already dressed in their swim clothes. Hope's heart races as she is surrounded by her family, though she is uncertain whether it is from excitement, fear, coffee, or a combination of all three. She reaches for her favorite double chocolate cake donut and takes a big bite.

Eric wipes away donut crumbs and his milk mustache with a napkin. "Aw, Mom, you're not even dressed yet."

Hope continues to chew but dramatically slower, wearing her best Mona Lisa smile.

"Give your mom a break, son." Matthew stands behind him and runs a hand through Eric's dark hair. "The water park doesn't open until ten."

While Hope takes her time getting dressed in her swimsuit and donning her cover-up, they are in line to enter the park with ten minutes to spare. As soon as the children are measured for their height at the entrance, Eric and Samantha run toward the nearest water slide, their bare feet smacking against the concrete.

"That was fast." Matthew laughs.

"Those two have already declared their undying devotion to Rachel for suggesting this place, and they've never even met her."

After getting their towels, the couple claims a centrally located group of loungers for the day. Matthew watches Hope as she settles in, placing a towel on four of the seats and emptying a backpack filled with four insulated tumblers.

"Did you bring the kitchen sink too?" he jokes.

Hope pulls out a thick book, one she began reading during the long drive to the resort. She smiles at him as she places it on a small table beside the nearest lounger. Then, with a flourish, she takes out her cellphone and earbuds.

"But, wait," she exclaims. "There's more!"

Matthew places a hand on her arm. "Hold it right there, Mary Poppins. Before you pull a lamp out of that backpack, you need to know that I intend to keep you in the water. All. Day."

Matthew removes the backpack from her and grabs her, embracing her in a bear hug, smashing her face into his chest. "Time now for you to learn something new."

Hope breathes in his scent and enjoys it before chlorine and sweat can mask it.

Releasing her, Matthew lowers his gaze to her. "Why don't you start by losing that cover-up and the flip-flops?"

As she pulls the cover over her head, she asks. "Shall we start with the kiddie pool?"

Matthew laughs, takes her hand, and tugs her along. "Not quite. But I think a nice round or two or three on the lazy river is called for."

Little by little, the water park fills with children of all sizes and colors. Adults of different ages stand and splash among them. The merriment grows louder, with shouts and laughter echoing throughout the vast space. The sharp whistles of the employees standing guard punctuate the air every so often.

Hope and her husband float together on the lazy river, each on a tube, holding hands as children bump into them or wade through the water around them. Matthew pulls her toward the exit with him.

"Time for something a little more triggery."

"I don't think that's a word, dear." Hope's hair is

still dry, but her wet swimsuit clings to her. They stand, dripping water from their suits, as their children run to them.

"Mom, Dad!" Samantha grabs Hope's hand. "There's a wave pool. Let's go!"

"Ohhh, I don't know," Hope says, planting her feet, resisting her daughter's tug. "Maybe your dad—"

Matthew takes her other hand. "That's exactly what I had in mind. Definitely more triggery."

The pool features a subtle, beach-like incline with beach chairs arranged in front of it. The depth varies from zero to just covering the toes, gradually extending to a full five feet of water. Little ones wearing water wings sit in the shallow area in front of the chairs, and Hope steps gingerly between them. Children bob next to their adults as the water gets deeper. Hope chooses to stand halfway in, with the water just below her waist. Matthew remains beside her while their children swim close to the pool's deeper end. A horn sounds, and the waves begin. Hope smiles as she watches her children delight in the waves gaining momentum.

Hope is aware. She is aware of her feet on the floor of the pool. She is aware of the feel of the water surging against her legs. Aware of her husband's hand in hers. Aware of the warmth in her chest and the peace in her heart.

The waves sway their bodies as if attempting to knock them over. But Hope stands firm, the grin on her face as permanent as her love for her life.

Snippets of a song enter her mind. Amy Grant sings about angels. *I know what you mean, Amy. I know what you mean.*

The water calms once again, and Hope meets

Matthew's gaze. The warmth she finds there makes her vision swim. He squeezes her hand.

"I'm so proud of you," he murmurs.

Hope beams. "Thanks. I'm proud of me, too."

Each time the waves cease, the two of them inch a little deeper. Hope allows the waves to lift her off her feet with delight. She focuses on how the water embraces her, like an old friend. After several rounds of waves, Eric swims to them and whips his wet hair from side to side.

"Mom, I'm hungry."

"Oh?" Hope peers about. "Maybe it is lunchtime." She takes her son by the hand as they move away toward the concrete beach. "Let's go see if the kiosk is serving yet."

"Where are you going?" Matthew asks.

"Somebody's hungry." Hope answers over her shoulder.

"Okay, wait up. Sam? Come along, honey. Let's go with Mom and your brother."

They eat. They lounge for a while. Eric points to a large striped apparatus nearby. "There's a big slide right over here. They call it the toilet bowl."

"Do you like it?" Hope asks.

"Well, it's kinda lame. But Sam likes it."

Samantha sticks out her tongue at her brother. "You just like saying 'toilet bowl.'"

"Do not."

"Do too!"

Eric smacks a hand on his sister's arm, smiling. "Last one to the toilet bowl's a rotten egg."

Then her children are gone again. Hope reaches for her book, but Matthew interrupts her.

"Let me stop you right there, my little bookworm. We can't let you dry off so soon."

"But—"

"No. Now, what do you want to try next? Want to take a whirl on the toilet bowl?"

"Want to play basketball in that pool over there?" Hope points in the opposite direction.

"What, with those third graders, who are only now learning multiplication?"

Hope rolls her eyes and stands with her feet planted wide, her fists on her hips. "Surely, they're old enough to know long division."

"But, honey." Matthew places an index finger under her chin. "There are four different water slides. We can start with the pre-algebra slide first, then make our way up to the calculus slide."

Then Matthew holds out his hand. Shaking her head, she gives him a lopsided grin as she takes it. "You're irresistible, sir."

The lines are long, but not long enough for Hope to lose her confidence. Once there is only one person in line before them, Matthew turns to her. "Do you want me to go first?"

"Yes," she answers. "That way you can catch me when I reach the bottom."

The attendant signals to Matthew to get into position. "Wait for the green light," the young man instructs.

Hope focuses on her breathing. She imagines D'Wayne's stick figure drawings. Where is she now? Which of those stick figures best represents her current awareness?

As Matthew disappears into the tunnel of the

water slide, she wiggles her toes. Then, she lowers herself onto the slide, gripping the sides of the entrance with her hands.

She is aware.

She waits for the light to change from red to green.

"Okay, you can go."

Hope pauses. She digs deep inside herself to find the warmth. She closes her eyes. *Angels.*

"Thank you," she whispers. Then, she crosses her arms over her chest and lets go. She closes her eyes as she whooshes down the slide. A smile spreads wide across her face as she flies out of the tunnel slide and splashes into the pool. Matthew is waiting in the pool for her, ready to catch her or grab her, if need be. She jumps into his arms.

"I'm ready for more of that!" Hope gasps, breathless with excitement.

Later that evening, when the children have fallen asleep, Hope and Matthew sit closely on the couch. Even though it is June, they light the gas fireplace, and Hope, cradled in Matthew's arms, gazes into the flames.

"Thank you for today." Her voice is low, but Matthew squeezes her to let her know he heard her. "If you'd told me even three months ago that I'd be standing in a wave pool or heading down a water slide, I'd have told you you were crazy."

"Did you have fun?" Matthew whispers in her ear, his voice soft and breath warm.

Hope reflects on her reaction the last time they were in a hotel pool. She thinks back to the times she stayed in the hotel room or went shopping while

Matthew and their children enjoyed swimming. How much she has missed. She reaches for Matthew's clasped hands across her chest. She definitely felt a sense of accomplishment. But did she have fun?

A tear squeezes out of her eyes. She whispers, "Yes. Absolutely."

Chapter Twenty-Five

The LORD is my light and my salvation; whom shall I fear? The LORD is the strength of my life; of whom shall I be afraid?
Psalm 27:1

John Wesley
Hayle Estuary, England
1786

While the swaying of the carriage had the potential to make reading fine print difficult, John managed to do so. He regretted the end of his days riding his horse all over England. However, taking a carriage made reading a bit easier. He had fallen from his horse more than once while reading a book. As if it remembered the falls well, his left hip began to ache. Rubbing it, he reflected that not only was his beloved niece, Sally, but his steed as well were likely relieved when he finally agreed to use a carriage.

Switching to a carriage had not decreased the number of miles he traveled, however.

As a gentle breeze fluttered the pages in his hand, John gazed out the open carriage window at the Cornwall countryside. Two horses pulling his carriage in the hands of an experienced, knowledgeable driver, ensured that he made better time than when he traveled alone on his single horse. He had hired his current driver from the London Inn in Redruth, someone familiar with the nooks and crannies of the route to St. Ives, where he had an urgent appointment that evening.

Every opportunity to preach was important. As the Methodist movement spread, he was invited all over the Great Isle to speak. The class meetings were essential for nurturing the faith of the adherents. He felt gratified that the Anglican Church transitioned from being exclusively for the elites of society to a revitalized body of Christ. Naturally, this created tension within the church. That was only to be expected. The upper echelon always got nervous when an institution flourished from the grassroots. Even more astonishing, the movement had reached across the Atlantic and was thriving there without the strict oversight of Anglican leadership.

Wesley's primary concern, however, was to support the growing movement on this side of the ocean.

As they approached the eastern coast at Hayle, the winds picked up, blowing the scent of Celtic Bay through the carriage. As John inhaled the sea-salty air, he was flooded with memories. He smiled as he recalled those horrific storms at sea many years prior. How he had cowered below deck in the murky dark, sick with fear.

The crash of waves hit John's ears. It must be high tide. The wind and the water created such a ruckus that he could barely hear his own thoughts. The carriage slowed to a stop. What in the world?

Wesley leaned his head out of the window. A man, a sea captain by his dress, clasped his tricorn on his head and stood next to the driver.

"Hullo!" Wesley shouted above the crashing water. "Why are we stopped?"

The captain glanced at him and shouted back. "The water... at its height... I... wait it out."

Wesley craned his neck toward his driver, who leaned toward the captain. The horses stomped and whinnied, and John smelled their fear. A passage of scripture came to him as he contemplated the captain: Acts chapter twenty-one. When Saint Paul reached Caesarea and stayed in the home of Philip, a prophet named Agabus visited to show the apostle what would happen to him. It was nothing Saint Paul did not already know. Was this sea captain Wesley's own Agabus?

Despite the wind whipping around them and the chilly sea spray, a warmth enveloped his shoulders. Deep within, a sense of peace and understanding resided. He smiled broadly at the sea captain but deliberately turned to his driver. The man angled his body toward him, his face full of inquiry: raised eyebrows, gloved hands gripping the reins, mouth held straight.

Wesley thrust his left hand out the window, pointing ahead. "Take the sea, man! Take the sea."

The sea captain scowled and shook his head. The driver's mouth opened, but John did not wait to hear any possible argument. He pulled his arm and head back inside. The carriage lurched and moved forward once more, and John leaned against the back wall. He resumed re-reading his sermon, but water splashed through the open window on his right, and he feared it might ruin the pages. After tucking it safely away in his bag, a question arose in his mind. It felt as though he were sitting on the seat next to his driver. John tilted his bare head before pushing it out of the carriage window again and shouted to the man.

Wesley's shout startled the driver, who was urging the horses onward. The driver turned toward him. "Sir?"

"What is your name, driver?" John had to raise his voice over the noisy elements, as practiced as he was in speaking over riotous crowds.

"Peter, sir." The driver gave him a look of disbelief.

"Peter, fear not!" With distinction, Wesley shouted his words. "Thou shalt not sink."

Once more, John settled back into the carriage as it meandered forward. His head was soaked with sea spray, causing the water to run down onto his shoulders and his long white hair to cling to his face. Wiping some of the hair away, Wesley smiled again, laying his head back against the wall.

At one point, John was certain that the water swirled around his feet, even seeping into the carriage. Moments later, the carriage wheels scrambled onto solid ground once more. Soon, the carriage came to a stop again. Peter's face appeared at the window.

"Are you all right, sir?"

"Of course, Peter. And you?"

The driver shook his head. "I am soaking wet. But you were right. We did not sink."

"Then, make haste, Peter. We must not dawdle."

After they arrived in St. Ives, Wesley directed

Peter to a tavern inn. There, they relieved the horses, and the two soaked men sought lodging. John procured warm clothes for Peter and ensured he was fed and warmed by a fire, noting that he only had enough time to make it to his appointment. With his hair still dripping onto his collar, he apologized to the owner for the Celtic Bay puddle on the tavern floor and took his leave.

He would arrive at the chapel to deliver his message with a few minutes to spare.

Chapter Twenty-Six

Faith, mighty faith, the promise sees,
And looks to God alone; Laughs at
impossibilities,
And cries it shall be done.
Charles Wesley

Hope
End of June, the Sunday of her final Sunday School lesson

"And what did the Apostle Paul have to say about it?" Hope sits at the round table, surrounded by her Sunday School class.

The spring daylight streams through the curtained windows, warming the room. She meets Mr. Hamilton's smiling eyes across the table from her.

"If you will refer to the worksheet, I have some New Testament passages attributed to him." Hope turns to the classmate on her right. "Janet, will you take the first one from First Corinthians? Then Terry, the second from Romans? Maybe we can go around the table from there. I'll give you time to find them and read over the passages to yourselves."

The class members thumb through their Bibles

and take turns sharing their assigned scriptures.

"Great, thank you." Hope spreads her arms. "What do you think, then? What were Paul's beliefs and attitude toward death?"

"He certainly wasn't afraid."

"Good, I agree with you, Terry. Why do you think he had no fear of death?" Hope nods in encouragement. Their discussions have been lively and full of thoughtful insights throughout their study so far.

"He knew the glory waiting for him."

"He had hope."

"He had already died once before and returned to the land of the living." Mr. Hamilton's answer causes some open mouths and cocked heads. "Remember, he was stoned and dragged out of Lystra's city gates, in Acts, chapter fourteen. Then he writes about being caught up in the third heaven in Second Corinthians."

Hope smiles at her former principal. "Thank you. That's a great point. Most likely, Lazarus wasn't afraid to die, either, having already gone through it."

"But I think hope is the key."

She can smell Janet's perfume from where she sits, the sweet vanilla scent that many ladies in that age group favor. "Hope for what, Janet?"

"To be with Jesus when we die. Hope that we will see our loved ones again. Hope in everlasting life."

"Great discussion." Hope stands and flips through some papers on the table. She holds up a picture of a ship on the open sea, tilting in violent, dark waves. "Remember when we read about Wesley's storm at sea?" She passes the picture around the table. This artist's rendition perfectly serves its purpose, with dark clouds, high waves, and the ship angled precariously.

She sensed that it accurately depicted what it must have been like for those on board that day. "Remember John Wesley cowering in a corner, terrified that he would die?"

They all acknowledge the memory of the story, and Hope grins at them. She locks eyes with Debbie, who leans forward. Hope is certain that every soul in the room remembers her panic attack weeks ago at the mere mention of the storm at sea. Debbie gives her a slight nod. Hope clasps her hands. "Well, then, get a load of this."

With sweeping gestures, gesticulating with her arms and moving her body back and forth, Hope tells the story of John Wesley and his driver, Peter Martin. She holds imaginary reins and lowers her voice to as manly a tone as possible to mimic the two men and the sea captain. She scowls as the captain might have at Wesley for ignoring his warning to turn around. Hope shouts out to an imaginary Peter Martin, stretching her neck as if hanging out of a carriage window, then cupping a hand to her mouth and calling at the top of her lungs, she bellows. "Take the sea, man! Take the sea!"

She finishes the story, leaving the class with an image of a dripping-wet Wesley leaving the tavern to go preach. Hope pauses, locking eyes with each class member in turn before she poses the question.

"How did John Wesley go from..." She grasps the picture of the storm-tossed ship. "From this, cowering in a corner deep within the ship's hull. To that? To calmly encourage his carriage driver to let the swimming horses bear them across a flooded road?" The room is silent. In the distance, muffled children's singing voices and the tinkling of the upright piano used for the children's Sunday School drift toward them.

Still standing, Hope again spreads her hands. "Is there any other answer than the one Janet gave us? For what is faith, but the 'assurance of things hoped for, the conviction of things not seen'?"

Hope falls into her chair. "Ladies and gentlemen, that concludes our six-week study of John Wesley and conquering the fear of death. Debbie has been preparing for our next study, which starts next week."

"And now for something completely different," Debbie mutters.

The classroom empties, leaving Mr. Hamilton, Debbie, and Hope behind. Mr. Hamilton extends a hand to her, and she takes it.

"Well done, Hope. You did such a better job than I would have."

She shakes her head. "No, sir. You still know the subject matter far better than I do."

He gives her a small smile, his eyes warm. "I have heard that story, the one about taking the carriage over the flooded estuary. It was a great ending to the study."

"Thank you, sir." Hope drops his hand. "And thanks for insisting I do this. I wanted to quit so many times."

His smile fades as he lowers his voice. "I had a sense that you needed to do it."

He leaves the room, and Debbie hangs behind as Hope gathers her papers. "He's right, you know."

"Mr. Hamilton?"

"Yes. God wanted you to do this."

Hope lets out a short laugh. "I think maybe John

Wesley wanted me to do it. Anyway, friend, we're done, and it's your turn. If I had a baton to hand off to you, I certainly would."

"Yeah, thanks." Debbie walks to the door, speaking over her shoulder. "I gotta try to top that."

Hope laughs and follows her friend. As she is about to pass the picture of the hand thrust into the water hanging on the wall, her face transforms into a crooked grin. She kisses two fingers and then touches the picture before exiting the classroom.

The sounds of the depths roar in her ears as the lake engulfs her. The water presses against her, and her hair entangles around her face. Her arms frantically push against the swirling darkness. The sudden cold of the water envelops her. Disoriented, she sinks. Which way is up?

She kicks her aching legs slowly. Needing air, she fights the urge to gulp the cold water, to extinguish the burning in her chest.

Her heartbeat slows. Think. Bubbles. Bubbles go upward. Her nostrils are full of water, though. The urge to breathe intensifies, and panic surges once again.

Look up.

Where is up? She sweeps her head from side to side.

Look up.

She tilts her head back. A beam of light shimmers above, diffusing through the water. She kicks, reaching toward it.

Warm, strong hands encompass her body, forcing her toward the surface. She is accelerated in her ascent against the pressure. The light radiates directly above. She is almost there.

Before she breaks the surface, she sees two distinctly different hands reaching for her. The first is a feminine, aged hand adorned with her Nana's signature fingernail polish. The other is a masculine hand, featuring neatly trimmed nails, framed by a white ruffled cuff extending from the black sleeve of a cassock. She reaches toward them with both arms, gripping the hands of her rescuers firmly as she is pulled out of the water.

Chapter Twenty-Seven
*I am not afraid of storms, for I am learning how
to sail my ship.*
Louisa May Alcott

Hope
Lake of the Ozarks, Missouri
Five Years Later

The unseasonably warm air whips Hope's stray hairs across her face, and she reaches to hold them back. Her job is to observe the skiers plowing behind them while Matthew drives their ski boat. She smiles as her son maneuvers out of the boat's wake, his strong arms gripping the tow line. She didn't mind one bit when Eric asked to bring his girlfriend along. Hope and Matthew both like this girl, and Hope knows full well he hopes to impress her with his skills on the water. They allowed Samantha to bring a friend for their lake outing as well. They assured the other parents that there would be no alcohol, at least not in their rented condo or on their boat.

Matthew takes boating safety very seriously.

Which is much more than she can say for the other boaters. Even though they have a couple more weeks before Memorial Day weekend, they pass plenty of coves filled with boats tied together. The weather forecasters were right—it's a beautiful weekend on the lake.

Hope glances back at her husband. His grin widens as their eyes meet, warming her chest. This is exactly what Matthew has always desired for their family. A pang of misgiving for all the years wasted hits her, and she turns back to keep an eye on her son.

If only fear had not stolen the time from her. But this is no place for regret. Matthew has insisted on this: she has more than made up for lost time. Hope is proud of her accomplishments. The swim class was so successful that she went on to become an instructor herself. Muscle memory took over, combined with the peace of the Holy Spirit, and she once again took to the water like a fish. She even fulfilled her childhood dream and took lifeguard classes, becoming certified. Had it not been for D'Wayne and his classes, she would still be holding her family back from enjoying their time together. On the water, where they should be.

Hope smiles. If Debbie were here with them, she'd remind her friend that it was actually John Wesley who set her on this course. John Wesley and his fear of death, his fear of storms, and his fear of perishing before seeing his mission come to any kind of conclusion. And Debbie would be right. Thank God for Reverend John Wesley.

Their boat is followed by a few teenagers on jet skis, taking advantage of the wake that Matthew is creating. The roar of their engines accentuates the sound of their watercraft crashing into the waves. They remind her of the photos she has seen of birds perched on the backs of rhinoceroses, feeding while cleaning the bugs off the animals. The mental image makes her smile, even though she's unsure whether there's any benefit for the boaters. They're more like turkey vultures cleaning up roadkill, now that she thinks about it.

Hope laughs aloud at the thought, though her laughter is drowned out by the commotion around her.

"How's he doing?" Matthew shouts the question at her.

She turns back to her husband. "He's doing great!" She gives him a thumbs-up in case he can't hear her.

Matthew nods before turning his attention back to the expanse of water before them. It's only a matter of time before the strain on Eric's shoulders forces him to drop the rope, so his parents wait out their son's bravado for his girlfriend's sake.

Hope notes that it has darkened. She turns her attention to the sky, frowning. Nothing but full sun and fluffy white clouds has filled the sky since they awoke this morning. She watches as a small gray cloud obscures the sun directly above them. Hope scans the rest of the sky, but no threatening clusters of clouds are visible. Just moments later, the sun re-emerges, and Hope observes that the tiny gray cloud moves lazily along.

The drone of a nearby boat catches Hope's attention, and she watches it pass by. Her girls wave to the other boaters. Hope smiles as an older woman, her hair flattened by a floppy, wide-brimmed hat, drives. Hope waves as well, noting a teenage girl leaning over the side. Hope's smile fades. A grandmother and her granddaughter? Nana's face jumps into her mind. Hope rises, as if in a dream.

Her son releases the tow line. Hope taps her husband on the shoulder. "He's down," she shouts.

Matthew promptly decelerates. He turns to note that Eric is bobbing in the water, his skis pointing up toward the sky. As he steers the boat in an arc to retrieve their son, Hope turns back to the presumed grandmother and granddaughter duo.

Time stands still.

Hope rises to her full height. The teenager is not in the boat, yet the older woman continues to drive. Hope studies the churning water where, just moments before, she had seen the teenager leaning over the side of the boat. The girl had not been wearing a life jacket.

You know what you must do.

Hope recognizes that 'strange warmth' within her, and, almost like a whisper, she hears the words from the Book of Esther, the ones spoken to Esther by Mordecai that Pastor Dave had paraphrased at dinner a few years earlier.

Maybe this is the very reason, just like Esther, for which you were created.

She places her bare foot on the edge of the boat as it turns.

Your will be done, Lord.

Full of confidence that God is with her and without a second thought, using the momentum of the boat's movement, Hope launches into the still-cold water of the lake.

THE END

Author notes

The first step of any twelve-step program is to admit one has a problem. My fictional character, Hope, has a problem. But she has 'dealt with it' for much of her life. As long as it only re-emerged around the anniversary of the accident and while she was sleeping, she felt it was manageable. How many of us suffer similarly? However, there had to be a trigger for her to understand that this was not something she could handle on her own.

All the contemporary characters, including Hope, her husband Matthew, their children, her friend Debbie, her church family, her therapist, and her pastors, are entirely fictional. The story of Hope was inspired by the true-life tale of Leslie Dennison, who died while saving her twelve-year-old granddaughter in 2018 under very different circumstances. Cognitive behavioral therapy (CBT) and EMDR (Eye Movement Desensitization and Reprocessing) are both real and effective forms of therapy. The swim therapy method that Hope and Debbie experienced is also genuine and is based on the technique created by Melon Dash. To learn more, refer to Dash's book Conquer Your Fear of Water: A Revolutionary Way to Learn to Swim Without Ever Feeling Afraid (2nd ed, 2022, by Brooklyn Writers Press) and the website miracleswimming.com.

Another great work that I often recommend to patients dealing with the sequelae of trauma (especially childhood trauma) is the book by Bessel van der Kolk,

The Body Keeps the Score (2014, Viking Press). It's an excellent resource for explaining the long-term effects of traumatic stress.

The stories of John Wesley contained in *Take The Sea* are primarily sourced from various biographies and his journal. I took total advantage of the gift from my pastor, John Shelton, of his mother's copies of The Works of John Wesley, 3rd edition, Complete and Unabridged, Volumes I-XIV, 1986, by Baker Book House, reprinted from the 1872 edition issued by Wesleyan Methodist Book Room, London. (I know you're jealous.) Other excellent resources for further reading include:

Heitzenrater, Richard P. *Wesley and the People Called Methodists*. Abingdon Press, 1995.

Leaan, Garth. *Strangely Warmed: The Amazing Life of John Wesley*. Tyndale House Publishers Inc, 1964.

Telford, B.A., John. *The Life of John Wesley*. Ambassador Publications, 1999.

Acknowledgments

Thanks be to God the Father, the Son, and the Holy Spirit (or the Holy Ghost, as John Wesley would say). Thanks to Susanna and Samuel Wesley for having so many children. Thanks to John Wesley for seeking God's will in his life, and to his baby brother Charles Wesley for his perfect lyrics, but especially for *O For a Thousand Tongues to Sing,* because it's my favorite of them all.

Thanks to ACFW (American Christian Fiction Writers) and its contests. The feedback I received from the First Impressions contest led to changes in the manuscript that made this work a semi-finalist in the 2024 Genesis contest. A huge thank you to all the judges. (I think I just wrote an entire paragraph without using a single exclamation point.)

Thank you, Janyre Tromp, editor and author. The misfortune that caused the two agents I had appointments with at the ACFW conference in 2023 to be unavailable resulted in my meeting you. I'm so glad I did. Ope, look. Another paragraph without an exclamation point.

Thanks to Cynthia Hickey, editor and author, and Winged Publishing for believing in me and this manuscript. I'll never forget how your eyebrows raised when I mentioned that this dual-timeline work includes

John Wesley.

Thank you to my book club, The Bluestockings, of Lebanon and Camdenton, Missouri. Abby, Amber, Brenda, and Stacey (who can find typos like nobody's business). You guys are the best! (Sorry, had to exclaim this.)

Thanks to my beta readers, especially Pastor Marsha Vincent and my sister, Beth Nansen.

A special mention of thanks goes to author Sarah Hanks (no relation to Tom or Abe Lincoln; I know because I asked) for her advice on all things dual-timeline.

Have you heard of Instagram? Thanks to all the bookstagrammers out there who are so encouraging to authors. Thanks to all my social media followers, friends, and family.

A big shout-out to Cira Monnig, FNP, who took care of my patients while my daughter, Amber, and I traveled to New Orleans for the ACFW Conference 2024. Of all the curly red-headed FNPs I know, you're my very favorite.

Thanks to my husband, Wes. He's the one who found and shared the story of Wesley crossing the high waters at the Hayle Estuary in England. While it's a really good story, nothing beats the Chicken Heart That Almost Ate Decatur. Thanks for believing in my writing and always being willing to be a first reader.

And thank you, dear reader, especially if you have read this far. I think you're pretty awesome, too.

Please leave a review on Amazon, Barnes & Noble, Goodreads, and BookBub. I appreciate you!